RESPONSE TO "MY FAMILY, THE J...

Norman Beim's recent colle...

A WALK AMONG THE FLOWERS:

"The dialogue was very well crafted, with a fine distinction between each of the characters. A lovely sense of rhythm and growth. The sense of memory is cleverly handled and very intriguing."

The Western Stage
Salinas, California

"Very realistic dialogue. Funny at times as well as poignant."

Black River Theater Company
Oberlin, Ohio

***

A ROSE OF SHARON

"I had a lump in my throat that was hard to get rid of and I hated to see it end. It was beautiful."

Soaring Eagle Productions
New York City

"The characters are well drawn and interesting, their relationships complex and their situation involving."

The Tennessee Repertory Theatre
Nashville, Tennessee

***

MY DINNER WITH MARK:

"Powerful material...a solid foothold on the characters."

Playwrights Horizons
New York City

"Deserves to be preserved, taped, played and kept at the Holocaust Museum in Washington...a marvelous writer."

Westport Country Playhouse
Westport, Connecticut

***

ZYGIELBAUM'S JOURNEY:

"Gripping piece of writing...powerful."

Wisdom Bridge Theatre
Chicago, Illinois

"Intriguing."

Royal National Theatre
London, England

"A very lovely piece"

Center Stage
Baltimore, Maryland

for Hymie,
the father I never really knew

NORMAN BEIM

Hymie and the Angel

A NOVEL

NEWCONCEPT press, inc.

EMERSON, NEW JERSEY

Library of Congress Cataloging-in-Publication Data

Beim, Norman
  Hymie and the angel/ Norman Beim
         p.   cm.
  ISBN: 0-931231-09-4 (trade paperpack: alk. paper)
  1. Jews--New Jersey--Newark--Fiction   I. Title.
PS3552.E4224H95 1999
813'.54--dc21   98-14194
                                                      CIP

Special thanks to LARRY ERLBAUM, ART LIZZA, FRANK BARA, MARVIN HAYES, RUTH ELY and last, but not least MARTY BEIM.

FRONT COVER DESIGN: HOMER GUERRA, New York City

Printed in the United States of America

10 9 8 7 6 5 4 3 2 1

CONTENTS

1 The Stranger 1

2 Death And Reprieve 14

3 The Beginning Of The Search 32

4 Tillie 43

5 Sunday Dinner 57

6 Uncle Sam And Aunt Rose 81

7 The Movies 95

8 Adam's Suit 103

9 Uncle Sam's Decision 111

10 Johnny Notte 119

11 Jack 125

12 The Letter 145

13 A Last Hope 155

14 Frieda 167

15 The Funeral 193

CHAPTER ONE

THE STRANGER

The morning rush was over. The nearby factory workers had been served their pre-work drink and the place was literally empty when the stranger appeared. Hymie had seen the stranger twice before, wandering about the street looking like a lost soul. The man was dressed shabbily, but there was something special about him. A sense of innate dignity, a certain air of refinement convinced Hymie that this was no ordinary tramp. The man came in through the swinging doors and came up to the bar.

May I have a glass of water? he asked.

Without a word Hymie picked up a glass, filled it with water and placed it on the bar in front of the man. The stranger picked up the glass, drank half the water and placed the glass back on the bar.

Thank you, he muttered and started out again, rather slowly.

Are you all right? Hymie asked.

And if I'm not?

Have you got a job?

Would I be wandering around the streets if I had a job?

Where are you from?

Not from around here.

He certainly wasn't the friendly sort.

If you clean up the back room you can help yourself to a sandwich. All the cleaning stuff is in the closet over there.

How about a sandwich first?

All right. That's the kitchen, right there.

You call that a kitchen?

It's got food in it.

Touche.

What?

Never mind.

That wasn't English. It sounded French, yet the man spoke without any accent. As he cleaned the bar, Hymie watched the man make himself a baloney sandwich.

This food isn't kosher, is it?

No.

So how come you're serving non-kosher food?

There aren't any Jews around here.

You're a Jew, aren't you?

3

I don't eat the food.

I'll bet.

Had the man been spying on him? Frieda (Hymie's wife) was a little bit of a fanatic, but she certainly wouldn't go so far as to send someone down here to spy on him. And how did the stranger know that he was Jewish? If he was a stranger, that is.

That's not bad baloney, as far as baloney goes.

I'm glad I passed the test.

Frieda kept telling him he spent too much on the food but you couldn't feed people slop, as some of his colleagues did. Even Goyim aren't dummies. Besides, it was different here in America. There wasn't that barrier between Jews and Goys as there had been in Poland. He had made deep and lasting friendships here among the Goyim. And as far as his sister, Tillie, was concerned she was more Goy than Jew. The stranger had gone into the back room and come out almost immediately.

That's quite a mess in there. What went on in there last night?

A wedding. You don't have to clean up everything. Just clean off the tables.

I don't mind.

The man filled the bucket with water, picked up the mop and some rags and went into the back room. The phone rang. It was Frieda.

Are you still angry? she asked.

No, I'm not angry.

Then bring home some milk! And she slammed down the phone. Obviously she was the one that was angry.

A few customers came in. Hymie served them, chatted with them and they left. He remembered the stranger and was about to go back and check on him when the man came out.

You've got a pile of garbage there. What do you want me to do with it?

There's a garbage can just outside the back door. Do you think you can manage it? (He did look sort of frail.)

I'll manage.

And the stranger returned to the back room. Hymie was curious and followed him. The place was immaculate. The tables had been cleaned off, the floor had been mopped and a neat pile of garbage had been gathered near the doorway. The man came back in from the outside with the garbage can.

Here, let me give you a hand, said Hymie.

I said I could manage.

Apparently the stranger was stronger than he looked.

You'd better go tend to your customer.

Hymie went out front. There was a customer standing at the bar. Now how did the stranger know that? He probably didn't. He just said that to get rid of him. That stranger was a strange one, indeed. And he didn't even know his name.

Do you want me to mop up in here?

Hymie whirled about. He wished that stranger wouldn't creep around like that. *No. I did it myself this morning.*

How about the kitchen? It's filthy.

The kitchen's fine.

Hymie was furious at the stranger for saying that in front of the customer. Thank God, there was only the one customer there. Frieda, herself, had said the same thing on one of her rare visits to the bar, but made no attempt to do anything about it since Hymie had made it perfectly clear that he would look after the business and she would look after the house. Hymie took the stranger aside. *What's wrong with the kitchen?*

The stove needs a good cleaning. As a matter of fact, everything needs a good cleaning.

Well, I can't afford to pay you for all this.

Food'll be fine.

But Hymie had the uneasy feeling that the stranger had something more in mind. A place to sleep, perhaps. That was out of the question. Not that he left any money in the register when he closed up, but the stock was valuable. He had quite a bit of liquor there. When the bartender, Phil, came in about an hour later the kitchen was gleaming.

Who's that?

He needed a job so I let him clean up around the place.

Better keep an eye on him.

Hymie said nothing. Coming from Phil that was rather ironic, since the bartender had very slippery fingers.

What're you doing, Buddy? Phil asked the stranger.

I'm making some sandwiches. My name is Adam. And Adam extended his hand, wiping it first.

Phil, said the bartender. He shook the stranger's hand, went behind the bar and put on his apron. *Looks like a college bum to me. What's his last name?*

I don't know his first.

It's Adam.

Adam? What kind of a name was that? The first man was Adam.
Was he Jewish? Not that it made any difference.

*Those sure are fancy sandwiches he's making. We're not gonna
sell all those, you know,* said Phil.

Hymie walked over to the kitchen.

How many sandwiches are you making?

There'll be enough.

That stuff gets stale. (Did I ask him to make sandwiches? Well,
maybe I did.)

I'm wrapping them in wax paper.

I can see that. It's almost gone.

There'll be enough.

What was this man's story? He seemed well educated, bright and
cheerful. Why was he wandering about the streets, apparently penniless?
One did read stories about millionaires pulling tricks like that. Frieda
was a good judge of character. He wondered what she would think of
him.

There! How's that look? asked Adam.

Beautiful, said Hymie drily.

And we'll sell everyone of them.

And they did. They had to send out for another baloney. When
the lunch rush was over Adam was quick to point out that the kitchen
sales had grossed quite a few dollars. When Hymie offered him some
money, to his astonishment, Adam refused it.

I thought you couldn't afford to pay me.

Well, you did bring in a little extra.

That's all right.

Hymie was beginning to feel very uneasy. He didn't like to be
in anyone's debt. And Phil was not too happy about it either. This guy
was setting a very bad precedent. He cornered the stranger a few
moments later.

Why did you turn down the dough?

The deal was for food, not money.

*Well, you may not starve to death but winter's coming soon and
you many need some warm clothes.*

*People worry too much about the future. It's human, I suppose,
but sometimes futile.*

Just as Phil thought. A college wise-acre.

I'm going, Hymie said as he got into his jacket. He turned to
Adam. *You can have whatever you want to eat.*

Thank you.

How was he going to dismiss this stranger? Did he want to dismiss him? He certainly came cheap. He decided to say nothing. *See you later,* he said, addressing no one in particular and strode out through the swinging doors.

Summer seemed loath to depart. The leaves were still on the trees. The sun was hot in the sky and children were still playing in the streets. He was all the way up Hawthorne Avenue when he remembered the milk. He couldn't understand why he had to pick up the milk. She couldn't send the boy? He didn't have enough to think about? Did she want one quart or two? He'd better get two. Tabatchnicks. That was as good a place as any.

He got out of the car and entered the dairy store. His nostrils were assailed by the pungent smells...pickles, sauerkraut, herrings, cheeses. Thank God he didn't have to wait too long. He drove slowly along Wolcott Terrace and turned left down Nye Avenue.

One twenty-four Nye Avenue. A two family house. The first one on the right, just below the corner. The hill had always bothered him. One time the kids had gotten into the car and released the brake. Thank God someone had seen it in time. He was sure he had locked the car. Was he getting absent minded? The children were nowhere in sight. He got out of the car, locked it and proceeded up the alley to the back door.

Did you get the milk? Frieda asked as he entered the kitchen.

Yes, I got the milk.

Frieda came away from the stove and they kissed perfunctorily. *Hang up your jacket.*

He wished she would stop treating him like one of the kids. There was a time, blessed in memory, when she had been a wife, and that was it.

Was there much traffic?

The usual. Where are the children?

Nathan's in the park with Irving and Harold, and Rachel's playing across the street. You're gonna wash your hands, aren't you?

Hymie went into the bathroom to wash his hands and relieve himself and he wondered what it was all about. Making money and raising kids, and a little bit of love. That was it. Not that he really craved that much more. Perhaps he was too content. His sister, Tillie, was a real go-getter, out in the car all the time with her suit club, new subscribers all the time. She even had her eye on politics. Well, he certainly put in the hours. No one could say he was lazy.

You gonna wear your coat at the table?

Hymie hung up his jacket on the coat rack and sat down to lunch.

What's the matter? she asked.

Why do you ask?

You're very quiet today.

I'm always quiet. It's the children that make all the noise.

She couldn't understand it. They were his children, too. They had been conceived in love, or what passed for love. As Frieda placed the soup on the table she looked at the man she had married. Had it been a love match? He had asked her stepfather for her hand that fatal day in Poland over fifteen years ago and been rejected. No one was good enough for her. But she had defied her stepfather, with her mother's encouragement, and here she was. He was in love with her, apparently, and she'd been friends with his sisters, and she wanted a home of her own. She had not been swept off her feet as she had dreamed she might be one day, and there were regrets. A saloon-keeper's wife. All right, she was a farmer's daughter, but surely she could have done better.

A transplanted Madame Bovary lost somewhere in Newark, New Jersey, she watched her husband eat his soup, all bent over. What atrocious table manners! She fiddled with the table cloth and some crumbs. If only he were a little more affectionate. There were some men who weren't afraid of exposing their feelings. Not that she was sloppily sentimental. She couldn't stand people that billed and cooed, and were kissy, kissy. But a little warmth now and then? What was wrong with that?

You ready for the meat?

The Neanderthal man nodded and she placed the meat in front of him.

Eat some bread.

There were always instructions, Hymie thought. Even in bed there were instructions. The meal finished, Frieda cleared off the table and started on the dishes.

I'm going to lie down.

Aren't you going to look at the paper?

Hymie was much too sleepy to read but he picked up the Jewish Forward and glanced at it listlessly.

Were you busy today?

We sold a lot of sandwiches.

Do you make any money on the sandwiches?

Of course, I make money on the sandwiches.

*I thought you provided them as a convenience. That's what you
told me.*

I make money on the sandwiches.

How much did you make?

I made a few dollars.

The children will need some clothes for school.

I should have kept my mouth shut.

So why didn't you?

You say I never share anything with you, so I told you.

How come?

This man came in and he fixed them up nice.

What man?

A man.

A man. What man?

A man. A stranger.

*A stranger? You let a stranger come into your place and make
your sandwiches?*

He was wandering around in the street...

Where is he now?

He's in the store.

You left him in the store? A complete stranger?

Hymie threw down the paper and strode into the dining room, sat
down on the daybed in the corner, which also served as a sofa, and
removed his shoes. Frieda followed him into the dining room.

Hymie, you're not serious.

What? What? What are you talking about?

*You invite a complete stranger into your kitchen and you leave
him there?*

What are you talking about? I do business with strangers.

But you don't let them behind the bar, do you?

Frija, please. I'm tired. Leave me alone.

But even as he spoke he knew the protest was useless. She was
off. With tears in her eyes she complained bitterly about his indifference,
indifference to his own flesh and blood, his irrational generosity to
strangers. No less dramatically, he reached into his pocket, pulled out
some bills and threw them on the floor.

You want my "neshuma"? Here take it!

Frieda   hesitated. She hated herself at these moments. Why
should she have to beg for money? She knew he had it and yet he made
her beg. She picked up the money and walked out of the room.

Hymie lay down on the daybed and turned his face to the wall. He patted the other pocket, in which he carried the bulk of his bills. How could a woman be so ignorant? She was supposed to be so clever, she and her brother, and yet in many ways she was stupid. He had to be left some dignity. Was he to face the world empty-handed? He shook his head at her obtuseness. She was still the little Polish Jewess that followed her husband across the ocean, full of fear and superstition. He loved her dearly for her weaknesses but when she clawed at him in her terror, and left him bleeding, he wondered how much longer he could go on.

In the kitchen Frieda counted her booty and sighed. Not as much as she had hoped, but it would have to do. How humiliating! She contemplated leaving him, for the hundredth time, but even to herself she couldn't lie any longer. Where would she go? What would she do? If only she were more like Tillie! More like a man. More self-sufficient. But she wasn't. She was a parasite. A helpless bloodsucker. That's what he had called her once, a bloodsucker. To have come to this. Begging for pennies from a saloon-keeper. She sighed again, pocketed the money and went about her housework.

Hymie woke suddenly to the sound of a ball banging against the outside wall. *Frija? Frija! What's that noise?*

Frieda rushed into the dining room. *What's the matter?*

What's that noise?

She opened the dining room window and stuck her head out. *What's the matter with you? Someone's trying to sleep.* And she closed the window. *You getting up?*

How can anyone sleep with all that racket? He slipped into his shoes and went into the bathroom.

What time are you going back?

Why?

If the children are back before you leave, I'd like to go to Springfield Avenue.

All right, so we'll go to Springfield Avenue.

But Nathan isn't back yet, and I don't want to make two trips.

So we'll go tomorrow. Is he still in the park? Even as the words came out of his mouth he regretted them. She was beginning to worry about the boy already. He could see that absent-minded look in her eye. Indeed, it was seldom absent.

Do you want something to eat?

I'll have some coffee.

I have your sandwiches all ready.

He wondered what things would have been like if the children had never come. Would they have been any happier? She had always been full of fear, especially after the war years. She carried her scars inside her like medals. It's true they had been harrowing times, but those days had long since gone. For him they had, at any rate. Who had time to brood about the past? Besides, the present was so much more gratifying. I mean, after all, when you came to think about it, he was riding high. He had married the woman who had struck his fancy. He had two beautiful children, and he had his own business which was beginning to prosper. He was an American business man and he had never even gone to school here, except for a few night classes in English. And here he was. The realization was a heady one. Each day was an adventure, each hour a challenge. He would wrestle with the future and carve out success. After all, in the entire world, who was more powerful than an American businessman? The American entrepreneur sat erect at the kitchen table waiting for his coffee.

Would you like a piece of honey cake?

He nodded stiffly. She brought out the precious honey cake, which she had managed to bake, God knows when. You think he appreciated it? How many women baked anymore? She cut a large slice and he devoured it without a word.

Send that man away, please.

It took him a few seconds to remember to whom she was referring. *Suppose I told you he was Jewish?*

Please!

There's something about him.

Everybody knows a few Jewish words.

I have a feeling about him.

Frieda dropped the subject. She knew when she was defeated. *You want some more cake?*

Hymie shook his head, rose from the table and put on his jacket. Frieda debated about whether she should say something about his drinking, but decided not to. They kissed and he left.

Hymie felt strangely tired as he drove through the familiar streets. A sadness crept over him. Summer was coming to an end. Was that it? The days were getting shorter already. His son's face appeared to him in his imagination. Her son's, to be exact. And then he envisioned the little girl. She was still partially his. Down the tree lined hills of Nye Avenue he drove, passing Goodwin Avenue, Osborne Terrace, down to Bergen Street. They had lived on Bergen Street a number of years ago. He waved to his friend, the proprietor of the butcher shop on the corner, and then turned left onto Bergen Street. There was the house they had lived in, the house to which they had first brought Nathan home and then Rachel. How proud he had been, and Frieda had been truly his. And now he understood things about his own parents so much more clearly.

His mind wandered back to the country roads of Brostek. He had returned there alone, a few years ago, because his father was dying. He had arrived too late, even for the funeral. They had borrowed money for that trip, one of the few times. But that was over, thank God. The death, the debts. Let's hope for good.

There was his uncle's tavern, the sight of his first job in America. He wondered how Uncle Sam was. He hadn't been in the best of health. Hymie drove along Raymond Boulevard, the railroad to his right, then turned and passed under the railroad bridge, back into home territory.

As he stepped through the swinging doors the room seemed different somehow, as if it had been newly painted. But that was nonsense. The smell of frankfurters filled the air. The stranger was at work in the kitchen.

What are you doing? asked Hymie.

I'm making hors d'oeuvres.

Another French world. *Nobody buys any food this time of day.*

I thought it might be good if we just passed them around.

For nothing?

They might drink some more.

Hymie frowned as he tied his white apron about his waist. *Don't use them all up,* he said. *Where did you get the toothpicks?*

They were on the shelf.

This man had fancy ideas, no doubt about that. The evening rush had started and Hymie had no time to think anymore about it. He was vaguely aware of the frankfurter bits being passed about on a plate with a little cup of mustard in the center no less. The evening rush seemed to go on forever. It was quite dark by the time the place emptied out for dinner. Adam smiled triumphantly. *They went pretty well,* he said.

Why not? They were free.

Phil said nothing. He watched the stranger sullenly and Hymie distrustfully. *I'm going,* he said, and he went home to eat.

That man steals from you. Did you know that?

I know.

So why don't you fire him?

He takes less than the one before. Have you had your supper?

I've had my dinner.

Where do you sleep?

I'll manage.

But the stranger made no move to leave.

You can't sleep here.

Why not?

At last it was out in the open. That's what he'd had in mind all along. *This is not a hotel.*

Without a word Adam went to get his jacket and put it on.

Where are you going?

What difference does it make?

You got any money?

None to speak of.

You looking for a job?

You offering me one?

You could help out in the kitchen, and we could use an extra hand behind the bar. When it gets busy, that is.

If I slept here, I could be your night watchman. What are you afraid of? Your bartender steals from you already.

The bar had been broken into twice last year. Did Adam know that?

All right. You can sleep here for now.

Hymie knew that Phil wouldn't like the idea, to say nothing of Frieda. But did she have to know? The hell with it! Fifty Bar And Grill belonged to him. It was his creation and he was the boss. So it was agreed that Adam could sleep in the back room. He had found the old cot in the closet and that was it.

CHAPTER TWO

DEATH AND REPRIEVE

When Phil returned to the bar that night after dinner he found the stranger still there.

You taking him on? he asked Hymie as he put on his apron.

We'll see, Hymie replied.

Phil said nothing more and tried to look indifferent as he went about his work. The stranger kept away from behind the bar but whenever Hymie caught sight of him he seemed to be busy doing something. As the night wore on Hymie became less and less observant. At one in the morning, after Phil had left, Hymie, in an alcoholic haze, began to lock up the place.

You want to show me how to set the alarm?

Hymie spun about almost falling to the floor. *Don't creep up on me like that!* he muttered.

I'm sorry, said the stranger.

Hymie stumbled about the place, giving rather incoherent instructions on how to set the burglar alarm. *You got that?* Hymie asked, none too clearly.

The stranger nodded.

I'll see you in the morning, Hymie said, trying clumsily to get into his jacket. *Where you gonna sleep?*

On the cot in the back room.

Right, right, Hymie mumbled and stumbled into the darkness. Where was the car? There it was. Had it been moved? No, there it was. The key didn't seem to work right. He finally got the door open and sank into the seat behind the steering wheel. He sat there for a while trying to regain his equilibrium. He finally shut the door, turned the ignition key and started the car.

He drove very slowly along the moonlit streets. Sometimes the car moved dangerously close to the center of the road and one time he came perilously close to a car coming from the opposite direction. The driver cursed as he passed him. At last Hymie reached Wolcott Terrace, turned the corner down Nye Avenue and parked the car in front of the house. Home safe.

He smiled vaguely as he stumbled out of the car, locked it and staggered up the alley. Just before he opened the outside door he remembered the mints in his pocket and popped one into his mouth. He walked up the three stairs in the back hallway very carefully but miscalculated the distance to the door of the apartment and bumped into it. He waited quietly, hoping he hadn't wakened Frieda, then took the keys from his pocket and opened the door. He closed it very gently and locked it. So far, so good. He closed the door to his and Frieda's bedroom and then the door to the children's bedroom.

It all seemed so unreal, so far away. A stranger in a strange land, a stranger in his own home. This was his house, wasn't it? And he was Hymie Bender, wasn't he, husband and father? Then why was he tiptoeing about like this? Why wasn't Frieda there to greet him? Why weren't the children there to welcome their provider? Hymie warmed the milk that Frieda had left on the stove for him, sat at the table and sipped it, nibbling on a roll.

Daddy, can I have some seltzer, please? Rachel's voice piped from her bedroom.

Hymie rose unsteadily, squirted some seltzer into a glass and brought it into the child.

Thank you, Daddy.

Shhh! Hymie cautioned.

Rachel drank the seltzer, kissed her father sleepily and turned back to her pillow.

Can I have some seltzer, too? Nathan's voice came from the next bed.

Hymie refilled the glass and brought the boy some seltzer.

Thank you, said Nathan, drank the seltzer, handed the glass back to his father and went back to sleep.

Hymie went back to the kitchen table and started to look at the Daily Mirror he had picked up earlier that evening. Frieda's door opened.

How long are you going to sit there? she asked.

I just got in, he replied.

Well, at least he wasn't falling down drunk. She went into the bathroom and came out very shortly. *You're falling asleep. Go to bed already,* she said and went back into the bedroom. Hymie continued to nod over the paper until he was asleep. Ten minutes later Frieda came into the kitchen and shook him awake.

What? What is it? Hymie looked up, rose, went into the bathroom and put on his pajamas.

Don't forget to brush your teeth, Frieda called.

Hymie brushed his teeth, came into the bedroom, got into bed and was fast asleep as soon as his head hit the pillow. Frieda lay awake, staring into the darkness and listened to Hymie snoring. She got out of bed, pulled the alarm on the clock and lay awake for another hour, contemplating her lot.

The alarm went off at a quarter to six but Hymie lay dead to the world. Frieda shook him. *All right, all right,* he muttered. But something was wrong. He didn't feel right. Frieda got out of bed, shut the alarm and put on her bathrobe. The mornings were getting chilly.

Hymie?!

Hymie grunted and lay there. Frieda went into the bathroom then returned to the bedroom.

Hymie!

Hymie stirred, sat up in bed and groggily placed his feet on the floor. Frieda went into the kitchen. When she came back into the bedroom Hymie was lying down again.

What's the matter with you? Are you all right? she asked.

Hymie muttered.

What? she asked.

I think I'm sick.

What's the matter with you?

I don't know.

You drank too much last night. What's the matter with you?

I'm sick.

I'll give you some bicarbonate of soda.

I don't want anything.

You're not gonna go to work? Who's gonna open up?

Call Phil.

You sure?

I'm sure.

Frieda called Phil, asked him to open the bar and said that Hymie would be in a little later. He wasn't feeling well. He didn't look well either. After the children had left the house and their bedroom had been straightened Frieda called the family doctor to make sure he'd be in. When she came back into the bedroom Hymie lay there, vacantly staring at the ceiling.

Is it your stomach? she asked.

I don't know. I feel sick all over.

He was just as bad a patient as the children. Worse. *You'll have to get dressed. Do you want me to help you?* she asked.

Hymie shook his head, sat up and slowly began to dress himself. Frieda was growing apprehensive. He looked very pale.

Do you think you can drive the car? she asked.

Hymie nodded. Frieda was dubious, but she didn't want to argue with him. The doctor wasn't that far away. She watched him nervously as they drove along Clinton Place. What a beautiful day it was! They parked right in front of the doctor's office. A few buildings away was the Roosevelt Theatre and Frieda noticed that a movie with Charles Boyer, one of her favorites, was playing there. Oh well, it would come to Hawthorne Avenue in a couple of weeks, hopefully on "dish night".

Frieda sat tensely in the waiting room as the doctor examined Hymie. She rose anxiously as he came out of the examining room.

What did he say? she asked.

Hymie shrugged and started out.

What did he say? she repeated.

He wants me to stay home for a few days, he replied.

He didn't tell her that the doctor wanted him to go into the hospital for a thorough examination, which was preposterous. Who could afford to go into a hospital? They stopped off at Goldman's pharmacy to fill the prescription the doctor had given him. Frieda fretted and said nothing. Suppose he did get sick, seriously sick. What would they do? They had no money to speak of, as far as she knew. How much could they borrow from relatives? What would become of them?

Don't worry. I'll be all right, he assured her.

She tried to smile but worried all the more at his reassurance. Suppose, God forbid, he were to die. It was ridiculous to think of a man so young dying, but it could happen. It was not impossible.

Oh, how she despised her weakness! She had been strong once, like iron. But no more. It was that goddamned war! It had broken her spirit. The responsibilities had been too much for her. At the enemy's approach her parents had sent her away to Prague, putting her in charge of her younger sisters and brothers. They had nearly starved to death. They had nearly frozen to death. How they had survived that winter she still didn't know. Back at the farm her mother had barely escaped being shot as she held the baby in her arms. And then there was that trip to Vienna, all by herself when she'd received word that Hymie, who was then her fiance and in the army, had suddenly been taken ill. She had fallen sick on the trip herself and almost died. After the war they had wanted to send Hymie to fight the Russians and that's when he'd fled to America. And that unforgettable trip across the ocean to join him in America. She'd spent most of that trip in her bunk, seasick, and homesick as well. She might never see her parents again, her brothers and her sisters. She still had nightmares about it all, and she hoped and prayed she would not pass on her "nerves" to the children.

Hymie had been through it all. He had seen his brother blown to bits before his very eyes and yet he seemed so calm, so steady, so callous. Men were so insensitive. Overgrown babies. She studied Hymie as he sat at the kitchen table.

So what are you gonna do? she asked.

I'm gonna go to work, he replied. *I can't leave Phil there all alone.*

Do you want me to come down with you? she asked.

He looked at her contemptuously. *You gonna serve the beer?* he asked. *You gonna wait on the customers?*

But if you're sick..., she replied.

So I'll get better.

And that was the end of that. Frieda regretted the times she had scolded him for no reason at all. *Take this soup along,* she said. *You'll heat it up. You have some bread there. Make yourself some toast. And call me. You shouldn't drive down there alone. Maybe Uncle Sam can take you down.*

I'll be all right, he said as he rose slowly. He took the bag of food and left the house. He felt awful. As he got into the car he noticed Frieda watching him from the window and he waved at her. He tried to smile. It was a feeble attempt.

He stopped and pulled over to the curb several times on the trip down. It was such a beautiful day. A summer day without the sweltering heat. A breeze caressed his cheek. He thought of Uncle Sam. Uncle Sam was often ill. How could he take it? It wasn't only the physical discomfort. It was this awful mental depression. Was it something he'd eaten? The doctor had been so vague.

He made a wrong turn and he cursed himself. He stopped the car for the fifth time and sat very still, waiting for the nausea to pass. His eye caught the rear-view mirror and a chill passed through his body. An inexplicable chill. A man was coming down the street. A dapper, well-dressed man with a goatee. The man was dressed in black and he seemed to be smiling as he approached Hymie's car. Did he know this man? The figure looked awfully familiar, and the smile. He'd seen that smile before. In his dreams? In his nightmares? In the trenches! Yes, that was it! That man had come for his brother once. Poor Yitzchok whose limbs were rotting away somewhere in Polish mud.

Hymie hastily started up the car, his illness forgotten. Beads of perspiration dripped down his forehead. The car moved slowly down the street. Too slowly, perhaps, but he didn't trust himself to go any faster. The black figure began to recede into the distance. Had he really seen that man? Or was it just an apparition? His imagination was beginning to play tricks on him. It was the illness. It was beginning to affect his brain.

He found himself on Hermon Street, parked the car and went into the bar. It was almost lunch time. The sandwiches were arranged neatly on a tray and Adam was behind the bar, working with Phil. Phil was smiling. He could hardly believe it. Phil never smiled. Adam was telling him a joke. They greeted Hymie warmly and asked him how he was feeling. Hymie was gratified by their concern, got into his apron and went to work behind the bar.

You look kinda pale, Phil remarked.

Hymie felt terribly weak but not as sick as before. Maybe he was beginning to get better. The noon rush began and Hymie prayed that he could see it through, but his prayers went unanswered. In the middle of drawing a glass of beer he suddenly felt nauseous. He almost fell to the floor. He set down the glass, muttered something to Phil and staggered into the back room. If he could only throw up. He sat in a chair, moaning softly. He didn't know how long he'd been there but when he looked up he saw Adam standing in front of him.

How are you feeling? Adam asked.

How do I look?

You look awful.

That's how I feel.

What did the doctor say?

He wants me to go into the hospital. Why was he telling all this to a stranger? But somehow Adam didn't seem like a stranger anymore. He seemed like an old friend, someone he'd known for most of his life.

Maybe you ought to go home. Phil and I can manage, Adam said.

Hymie shook his head. *I'll be all right. How did you do with the sandwiches?*

You'll be a rich man one of these days.

If I live. What time is it?

Three o'clock.

Three o'clock? Where did the time go?

Why don't you lie down? I'll call you when it gets busy, Adam said.

Hymie had no choice. He simply was not up to going back to work. Adam pulled out the cot and rolled up some rags in a towel for a pillow. Hymie muttered his thanks and lay down on the cot, resting his head on the improvised pillow. He lay there half asleep, half awake. Shadows played across the floor. Sunlight revealed rays of dust in the air. Voices from the bar floated into the room. He heard the phone ring in the distance. That was Frieda. Phil came into the room.

Your wife's on the phone. She wants to talk to you.

Hymie rose. It took all of his strength.

Can you make it? Phil asked.

Hymie nodded and walked slowly into the bar. It was almost empty. He picked up the phone. *Yes? What is it?*

How are you feeling?

Lousy.

Maybe you should come home.

What time is it?

It's almost ten o'clock.

I'll close early.

Don't drive home by yourself. You hear me?

I hear you, I hear you, he said and he hung up. Ten o'clock. Where had the day gone? Phil had done well for himself. He was sure of that.

How are you doing, Hymie? one of the customers called.

Hymie smiled weakly and waved at him.

That's what you get for drinking your own beer, another customer taunted.

Hymie tired to smile, nodded and moved slowly into the back room. Phil came in.

I'm going home. I don't think you'll need me anymore. Adam'll help you close up. You want me to open up tomorrow? Phil asked.

Please, said Hymie.

Take it easy, said Phil and he left.

Hymie sat for a while and tried to regain his strength. When he came back into the bar Adam was alone behind the counter.

How are you doing? Adam asked.

Hymie nodded weakly.

How about some soup? Adam asked.

Hymie shrugged.

I'll warm it up for you, Adam said and he proceeded to warm up Frieda's soup. Hymie sipped it slowly. He had no appetite, but he forced

himself. He finished half the bowl and pushed the rest aside. The light
in the bar flickered and Hymie felt a chill. Was there a draft somewhere
or was it just his illness?

What's wrong with the lights? Adam asked.

The fuse is going, said Hymie. *The fuse box is in the back, near
the outside door. I've got some extra fuses in the closet on the shelf.*

Adam left the room to take care of the lights. Hymie shivered
slightly. Where was that draft coming from? He heard the man's voice
before he caught sight of him.

Good evening, Hymie.

Hymie looked up to see the man in the black suit with the goatee
standing directly in front of him.

Who are you? Hymie asked.

We've met before.

I don't remember.

*You're to come with me. Your brother's been asking for you. You
remember Yitzchok, don't you? And your beloved father? They miss you,
Hymie.*

My brother's dead, and so is my father.

Some people have all the luck.

I have two young children, and a wife. They depend on me

I'm sorry, Hymie, the man in black said and held out his hand.
Come along.

*But I just got sick. An upset stomach. People don't die from an
upset stomach.*

*You'd be amazed at what people die of. Only yesterday a man
choked to death on a piece of bread. Isn't that ironic?! The staff of life.
Come along.*

I won't go.

I'm afraid you have no choice.

Keep away from me, said Hymie and he started for the baseball
bat which he kept behind the counter as a weapon for emergencies, but
he froze in mid-air. *I won't go,* he said. *I'll fight you and I'm not a weak
man.*

None of us are that strong, my friend.

*Just a few more years. Till the children are grown. That's not too
much to ask.*

I'm afraid it is.

But what have I done?

*My dear Hymie, look about you. Is this worth fighting for? A
dreary tavern in Newark, New Jersey? A wife who nags at you. Two*

*children who are almost strangers. You barely pay your bills. Your
bartender is stealing you blind. You'll never be a millionaire if you live
to be a hundred. The few animal pleasures...fleeting, momentary. You're
not a king. You're not even a philosopher. You're a speck of dust.*

I'm a human being, Hymie thundered and he rose to his full
height. *I was created by God. I am the seed of Abraham and Isaac and
Jacob. God, himself, spoke to my ancestors.*

He'll never speak to you, my friend, said this apparition in black
and moved slowly toward him, and then suddenly he stopped and stared.
Adam had entered the room. *What are you doing here?* the man asked
in amazement.

I might ask the same of you, said Adam.

I've come to fetch our friend here.

There must be some mistake, said Adam.

I never make mistakes. Well, hardly ever. He took a sheet from
his inside pocket. *Here we are. Bender, Hymie. Forty one.*

I'm forty, said Hymie.

*Newark, New Jersey. I assume, quite safely I think, that there's
only one Hymie Bender in Newark, New Jersey.*

How about a drink? On the house, said Adam.

Hymie looked at Adam with new admiration. How cool he was.
How calm in the face of Death. Obviously this Adam was not an
ordinary man.

J and B? asked Adam.

If that's the best you have, Death replied.

Adam poured a shot as professionally as if he'd been tending bar
all his life. Hymie knew that he must be delirious. This could not be
happening in his bar on Hermon Street. Death downing a shot of J and
B Scotch, and some obviously extraordinary man called Adam pouring
him a second one.

How long have you been here? Death asked.

Not very long.

What happened?

*We all make mistakes and, I suppose, I made more than my
share.*

What sort of mistake? I'm curious.

If you must know, I spoke out of turn.

What did you say?

*What difference does it make? I didn't like the way things were
run. Wars, plagues, etcetera, etcetera.*

You think you could do better?

Let's drop the subject. Shall we?

But Newark, New Jersey?

It's really not that bad. And Hymie, here, is a gentleman and a scholar. Well, a gentleman at any rate. And if one has to serve a human one couldn't make a better choice.

That was an interesting bit of news, thought Hymie.

Have another drink, Adam continued.

You're not trying to get me drunk, are you?

Moi? Don't be ridiculous.

How long you in for?

I'm not quite sure.

I thought you were a favorite.

Yes, well, even the Lord has his moods, said Adam and started to pour another drink.

That's all for me.

I may be in a position to do you a favor, you know.

It all seemed so crass to Hymie, so undignified. Did angels really talk like that? They were bargaining over him as if he were some piece of merchandise. Even in death there ought to be some dignity.

Sorry, said the angel of death.

Oh come, come.

Impossible. I've got my quota. You know that.

Suppose we find a substitute? asked Adam.

Hymie could hear his heart pounding. His head was throbbing as if it were going to burst.

A substitute?

Why not? What difference does it make to you?

The clock ticked loudly. Hymie held his breath.

No dice.

You're a gambling man. One throw. Hymie, where are those dice?

Uh, uh.

Why not?

How do I know those dice aren't loaded?

Okay. How about a hand of Black Jack? One hand? Come on. Just one hand.

Death sighed and shrugged reluctantly. Adam turned to Hymie and nodded. Hymie walked quickly to the drawer under the register, took out the deck of cards and handed them to Adam.

One hand, said the angel of death.

One hand, Adam agreed.

I cut the cards.

Adam handed over the deck.

And I deal.

It's a deal, said Adam.

Death shuffled the cards...very professionally, thought Hymie. Two cards were dealt to each of the players, one face up, the other face down. Hymie was so nervous he could hardly remember how the game was played. The object, of course, was to get closest to twenty one. Adam had a ten showing. The gentleman in black had a nine.

Another, said Adam.

Death dealt Adam a three. Adam now had thirteen showing.

I'll stick, said Adam.

Death thought for a moment then dealt himself another card, a four. They both had thirteen showing. Adam revealed his hidden card, a six. Death smiled and revealed his hidden card, a six. It was a tie.

One more hand and that's it, said Death and dealt another hand. Adam had a four showing and Death had a ten.

I'll take another, said Adam and Death dealt him a three. *Another,* said Adam. Death dealt him a two. *Another,* said Adam. Death dealt him a six. *I'll stick,* said Adam. He now had fifteen showing. Death revealed his hidden card, another ten, which meant Death had twenty. Hymie's heart sank. Adam revealed his hidden card, a six. Twenty one! Hymie heaved a sigh of relief.

Are you up to your old tricks? asked Death suspiciously.

Have you ever known me to cheat? And besides you were the dealer. You're holding the cards.

Okay, okay. What do you propose?

Give us a year to find a substitute.

No way.

Six months.

Three.

Make it four.

Okay, okay.

No, no! thought Hymie. At least six months. But he didn't dare say a word.

You've got until winter.

It's a deal.

Hymie sighed, but what could he do? Four months to achieve the impossible.

Would you care for a sandwich? Adam asked.

You must be kidding?

The menu has improved.

I'll see you in December.

Good hunting, said Adam.

Same to you, said Death and he chuckled, which made Hymie very uneasy. And he was gone.

Adam and Hymie were alone in the bar and Hymie was almost convinced that none of what he had witnessed had really happened. He was still sick, wasn't he?.

I'll drive you home, said Adam.

Hymie didn't have the strength to protest and, besides, if an angel offers to drive you home, do you say no? Adam turned off the lights, locked the doors, set the burglar alarm and helped Hymie into his jacket.

Who are you? Hymie asked.

Your private angel, Adam replied, his eyes twinkling.

But Hymie knew he wasn't joking. And why not? If a poor farm boy from Poland, a Jew, no less, could become an American business-man why shouldn't he also be blessed with his own private angel?

Hymie allowed himself to be helped into the car. He didn't remember giving Adam the keys but he must have since there they were, in the car and Adam was driving.

The car seemed to float through the night. Hymie looked at the moon and the dark tops of the trees. Everything seemed so unreal. The railroad embankment along Raymond Boulevard looked like some strange mountain on another planet. The diner on Frelingheysen Avenue looked like some monster spaceship. The open space at the lower section of Hawthorne Avenue with it's railroad tracks and factories in the distance, looked like some deserted expanse on the moon; and the deserted stores, as they drove up Hawthorne Avenue, looked haunted. It was an odd night indeed! How dark Wolcott Terrace was. The moon had disappeared behind a cloud.

As they pulled up in front of the house Hymie realized that he had not given Adam any directions. The lingering doubts vanished once and for all. Adam was definitely not human. But why had he, Hymie Bender, been chosen? Had he done something special? Hymie's head ached with all the questions that crowded into it. And the foremost question was, of course, had the bargain really been struck? Did he really have till winter to find himself a substitute?

Are you all right? Adam asked as they walked up the alley.

I'm fine, said Hymie and, indeed, he was feeling better.

Adam unlocked the kitchen door and allowed Hymie to enter first. Had Hymie given him the keys? *I'd better close the bedroom doors*, said Hymie and proceeded to do so. He then turned on the kitchen light and closed the outside door. *Sit down*, he said. *Sit down. Would you like some coffee?*

Please don't fuss, said Adam. *I'm here to serve you. I've been a wicked angel, you see, and that's my punishment. No slur intended.*

I'm not dreaming this then?

I'm afraid not.

Frieda entered the kitchen in a robe, perplexed and curious. *Hymie?* When she caught sight of Adam she stiffened and her eyes grew large with fear.

Riboine shiloilum! Who's that?

Don't be afraid, my dear, said Adam. *I'm not going to hurt you.*

This is Adam, said Hymie. *The man I was telling you about.*

Hymie, this is no ordinary man.

Your wife is very perceptive, said Adam.

She's very religious, said Hymie.

Why are you here? What have we done? asked Frieda apprehensively.

He saved my life, said Hymie and he told her the whole story. Frieda listened so calmly and so quietly that Hymie doubted whether she'd heard what he was telling her. *Did you hear what I said?* he asked.

You have until winter to live, she replied.

To find a substitute, he corrected.

Frieda said nothing. She just looked at Hymie as if he were dead already, which made Hymie very uncomfortable. She was convinced already that he would find no one to take his place. Dear, sweet Frieda. If a glass was half full, to her it was half empty.

Would you like something to eat? Frieda asked Adam. *I have a piece of chicken, if you like.*

Not now, thank you.

Some soup, maybe? Something milichik? A glass of milk maybe? A piece of honey cake?

Nothing, thank you. I'm a little tired.

Yes, of course. You can have our bed.

That won't be necessary. I can sleep on the daybed.

(How did he know they had a daybed?)

I'll get some sheets and a pillow, said Frieda.

Please don't bother. I don't need anything.

The door to the children's bedroom opened and little Rachel entered in her pajamas, followed by her brother. Without a word each child walked up to Adam and kissed him on the cheek. They seemed to be sleep-walking. Rachel then went into the bathroom, closing the door behind her. Nathan waited and when Rachel came out he went into the bathroom. They both returned to their room, closing the door behind them. Frieda sat quietly, lost in thought.

The sofa's right in here, said Hymie, and he led Adam into the dining room.

That'll be fine, said Adam and he sat on the sofa which doubled as a daybed.

Hymie returned to the kitchen, closing the door to the dining room behind him.

Did you give him some pajamas? asked Frieda.

Hymie shrugged and went back into the dining room. Adam lay fast asleep on the daybed. His face seemed to glow in the dark. Or was it just the moonlight?

He's asleep, Hymie said, back in the kitchen.

How are you feeling?

A little better.

Frieda felt his forehead. *You have no fever,* she said.

Hymie took her hand and kissed it. Frieda smiled. *Maybe you are getting better,* she said and went into their bedroom.

Hymie washed his face, changed into his pajamas and joined Frieda in bed. They lay awake until dawn, holding each other, each thinking their own private thoughts.

CHAPTER THREE

THE BEGINNING OF THE SEARCH

The following morning Hymie was wakened by the ringing of the phone. Frieda entered the bedroom all dressed.

It's Phil, she said. *He wants to know how you are. Do you want to talk to him?*

Why didn't you wake me?

You needed the sleep.

Hymie got out of bed and answered the phone.

Yes, Phil? What is it?

How are you feeling?

Much better.

Harry Waters is here. Do you want me to pay him? (Harry Waters was one of the beer salesmen.)

How much is the bill?

Forty-three ninety-seven.

Pay him and get a receipt. How did you make out this morning?

It was kinda slow.

I'll bet, thought Hymie.

What time you comin' in?

I'll be in for lunch.

See you later, said Phil and he hung up.

Maybe you shouldn't go in today, said Frieda.

And leave Phil all alone there?

Adam said that he was going down.

I need some aspirin, said Hymie and went into the bathroom, shutting the door behind him. He put down the seat and sat on the commode. He needed some time to think. His head was spinning. He still hadn't digested the events of last night. Had he really been approached by the Angel of Death? Did he really have until winter to live? It all seemed so impossible in the light of day. He was a religious man, not a fanatic maybe, but he was religious. But angels bargaining for his life? Was Adam some sort of a creep? Had the stranger put something in his drink that had made him ill and dream all sorts of strange happenings?

And then Hymie remembered Adam's sleeping head on the pillow last night, that unearthly glow. That had been no dream. But what

33

did God have in mind? With one hand He sends Adam down to earth to work for this saloon-keeper. With another He sends the Angel of Death to take him away? It didn't make any sense. Was God aware of what was happening? Were all these supernatural events merely accidents? Was there such a thing as a supernatural accident? And if last night was a reality, and it must have been, what about Frieda and the children? What about himself? Was he really doomed to die if he couldn't find someone to take his place? Soldiers found substitutes...for money, of course. Why couldn't he? But how much money did he have? And a substitute for a soldier was a little different from a substitute for certain death. He shuddered. He had faced death before, the possibility of death, that is, but there he'd had a fighting chance. Here there was no alternative. He had to find a substitute and that's all there was to it.

He brushed his teeth, shaved and was about to go to the table in his pajamas when he saw Frieda frowning at him. He went into the bedroom, put on his shirt and trousers and came into the kitchen for breakfast. Adam was sipping a cup of coffee, his second, apparently. Ridiculous! An angel drinking coffee.

You look pretty good this morning, said Adam cheerfully.

Frieda seemed to be completely charmed by the angel and Hymie felt a pang of jealousy. Idiot! Why should anyone be jealous of an angel? But he was, and Adam was aware of it because he smiled mischievously. Maybe this stranger wasn't an angel, after all. If he could drink coffee and he could sleep and he could eat, he was probably capable of other bodily functions as well. Hymie made up his mind to keep a sharp eye on him.

And now that he knew that Adam was an angel how was he supposed to behave towards him? He didn't want to fawn over him and make a fool of himself. On the other hand an angel was close to God and he didn't want to behave disrespectfully. The angel had assumed a human form so wasn't it logical to treat him like any other human being? Polite and respectful. That was the ticket. Adam was simply a man that was working for him, a man who was dependant on him for his livelihood, and that's the way Hymie was going to treat him, as just another employee. On the other hand Adam had saved his life. Well, not altogether. He'd obtained a reprieve. A postponement. A temporary postponement.

You look very thoughtful this morning, said Adam.

Wouldn't you?

I'm sure it'll work out all right.

Hymie looked Adam in the eye for reassurance, but Adam lowered his eyes. He wasn't so sure after all.

Hymie looked about him at the modest kitchen, clean but messy. Papers and dishes lying everywhere, and yet you could eat off the floor. It was just like Frieda's mind, cluttered, confused and utterly pure. Hymie ate his breakfast in silence. He was about to ask Adam for the car keys when he felt in his pocket, and there they were. He knew Adam had not returned them last night. Well, maybe he'd given them to Frieda and she had slipped them into his trousers pocket.

And suddenly all of Hymie's actions took on a new light. All of his surroundings were viewed through different eyes. His time on earth was limited and he saw everything with a dazzling clarity...his entire personality, good points and bad, and the same with Frieda. He saw his children so clearly, his little girl and his son. He saw how the quarrels he and Frieda had, had affected his offsprings, how the love he and Frieda felt for one another warmed their children as well. He had seen the world with just such clarity once before, when he'd faced death in the war. But then, as the years had passed, this keen perception had faded. But here it was again and it was blinding.

Are you all right? Frieda asked.

Yes, I'm fine, Hymie snapped absent-mindedly. It was all too much for him.

We've got a lot on our mind, said Adam to Frieda and he winked at her.

Adam could be very annoying with his cool superiority and his charm.

How easy it would be to just let go. No more worries. No more bills, no more cares. Life was so complicated. Was it really worthwhile? He didn't want to go back to the bar. He just wanted to sit at home with Frieda. How long had it been since they had made love? If only they could take a walk in the park, alone. No children, no business cares. Just the two of them and the trees and the sky and the fresh air. Hymie smiled at Frieda and she smiled back at him and kissed him.

Drive carefully, she said.

And he saw that her nagging was part of her love for him. After all, he wasn't so skillful at expressing his affection for her, was he?

Hymie drove back to the bar with Adam. It was a cloudy day and he felt depressed. Not only depressed but weak and helpless. He was a healthy man, a strong man. He was used to doing for himself. He was not accustomed to asking for favors. He realized now, more keenly than ever, that it was sometimes necessary to ask for assistance...a relative, a close friend. But he needed more than assistance. Hymie needed someone who was willing to give up his life for him. Why would anyone in their right mind do that? The hell with it! He couldn't think anymore. Maybe Adam could straighten things out if, as he claimed, he was God's assistant. They would have to sit down and have a long, long talk.

Back at the house Frieda's mind was in a whirl. She had gone through her daily tasks absentmindedly, the children's breakfast and some superficial cleaning and straightening. The children were off to school. She had entrusted Nathan to take his sister to kindergarten. There was the wash to do but that would have to wait. She had to think, think, think.

That morning had been an eye-opener. All this time she had taken her husband for granted. Oh, there were times, when he had a cold, for example, that she was concerned about him. But not seriously. Hymie was an oak tree, an anchor, a tower of strength. She was the fragile creature hemmed in on all sides by unnamed fears, threats to her sanity. But enough of that. That was all nonsense. This was reality. Or was it? Adam was real. She knew that. And if Adam was real so was Hymie's predicament. And a hopeless predicament it was! No! She mustn't allow herself to think like that. She would look on the bright side, on the side of hope, even if it killed her. The alternative was unthinkable. How could she survive in this strange country with two children to raise? Who would take her in? And even if she were to try to find some sort of a job, what could she do? And who would look after the children? Could she go back to Poland? Ridiculous! Her mother was getting old and wasn't that well herself.

And there was another thing, something she avoided thinking about. She was a woman now, with all the embarrassing things that went with it. There were times, to her chagrin, when she felt an attraction to another man. Not seriously, of course, but there it was. In that department Hymie was fine, not that she had anyone else to compare him to. At any rate, sitting alone in the kitchen with Adam, an angel mind you, she had started to blush. Unthinkable to have such feelings, subconsciously or not, toward an angel? What kind of a woman was she? And even stranger than that Adam had been blushing, too. For a moment she doubted his authenticity. An angel was an angel! How could he possibly...? At that moment the phone rang. It was Tillie, Hymie's older sister. They spoke every morning.

I can't talk long, said Tillie. *I've got a busy day.*

Thank God for Tillie. If anyone could cope with reality, if anyone could cope with the world at large it was Tillie. If Hymie was an oak tree Tillie was...the Eiffel Tower.

You were supposed to call me, Tillie continued. *Did you send off that package to Europe? Frija? Are you listening to me? Frija? Are you there?*

Yes, I'm here.

Is there anything wrong?

How to tell her. *Tillie...*

What is it? The children? Hymie? Frija, you're making me nervous.

It's Hymie.

He had an accident. I told him he shouldn't drive when he drinks. I told him a million times.

No, no. It wasn't an accident. Finally the words came tumbling out, incoherently at first and then she got hold of herself and went into all the details as clearly and precisely as she could. When she had finished there was silence at the other end of the line. *Tillie...? Are you there?*

I'm here, I'm here. And his name is Adam, you say?

Tillie, I swear to you...

All right, all right. What does he look like?

Nice.

Nice? What does that mean "nice"? Is he tall? Is he short?

Medium.

Blond? Black hair?

Brown. Light brown. Nice looking. Very sweet.

Nice looking?

Nice looking. Tillie, I don't know what to do? What shall I do?

Nothing.

Nothing?

Nothing. Leave it to me. Give me some time. Let me think.

You think you can do something?

He's a person, isn't he? This angel I mean. I mean he may be an angel, but right now, right here and now he's a person. And when it comes to people I know how to handle people.

How?

You've got to use psychology. If there's one thing I can do, Frija, I can handle people. I wanna have a talk with Hymie first. Bring him over to the store tomorrow. I'll be here till noon. No later than that. You hear me? What's the matter?

You know how stubborn he is. Maybe I shouldn't have told you.

What are you, crazy? My brother may be dead in a couple of months and you're going to keep it a secret? Please! I'm his sister, for God sake!

Tillie, I don't know. I really don't know. All I know is I'm a nervous wreck.

Forget your nerves. Be here no later than noon. You hear me?

I hear you.

Good-bye. And Tillie hung up. She sat perfectly still trying to collect her thoughts. Where was she? In the back of the store. Right. In the back of the store. Physically, that is. Mentally she was back at a farm outside of Brostek, a rustic village near the Polish/Austrian border. Images of her youth floated by. Her father with his dark, curly beard who had died just a few years ago. Her mother, working patiently. The dark woolen dress. The wry smile. The traditional wig covering the shaven head. And there were her sisters and her brothers. The youngest who'd died in the war and there was Hymie. Hymie as a darling infant. Hymie as a mischievous boy. Hymie as a shy young man, stubborn and proud and so handsome. She remembered embracing him when he went off to war. She remembered kissing him goodbye when she left for America, and then greeting him when he arrived at Ellis Island in New York, looking so confused and lost and so lovable. But he was stubborn. He didn't like to be beholden to anyone. Neither did she, for that matter, but there were times when you had to go out on a limb…to dare… risk disaster. After all, what could they do to you? There was no such thing as debtors' prison here in America.

She'd learned to make a place for herself in the world. She'd learned the hard way, ever since Morris had had that terrible accident and become a troubled cripple. The debts, the pain, the suffering. But she'd borne it all, taken it all on her shoulders, and she ran the clothing store almost singlehandedly. She was the mainstay, the support of two handsome boys, an ailing husband and a business that needed constant care, attention and nurturing. It was a continual struggle, and her suit club was a stroke of genius. Fearlessly she climbed into her car day after day, enrolling one member after another. Young and old. Poor and wealthy. She zeroed in on everyone. The ordinary man in the street, the firemen, the policemen, the police officers, the chief of police, lawyers, doctors, politicians. No one was to small or too big. They all wore clothes didn't they, they all put on their trousers one leg at a time and, at one time or another, they'd need a suit. She'd become a local celebrity and people hailed her as she drove by.

But there were times when she hated herself. Hated the humiliation she deliberately exposed herself to...hawking, wheedling, flattering. Whatever it took. But what choice did she have? They had to eat. She resented the burden she was forced to endure, but the sight of her two strapping sons gave her the courage and the incentive to go on. And where she found the time and the energy to cook and do some housework she herself never knew. And now there was Hymie. In addition to everything else, now there was Hymie, her beloved little brother.

She sighed wearily. How does one deal with an angel? That would take a lot of thought. But it was a challenge. And if there was anything that spurred Tillie on it was a challenge. She rose and entered the store. Morris was reading the newspaper.

That's all you've got to do? she snapped.

What do you want me to do?

She regretted the words almost immediately. Lately his leg had given him a great deal of pain. The heat treatments, the massages, nothing had been doing any good. They'd made an appointment with the doctor, much good it would do. But who else was there to turn to? She debated telling him about her brother's predicament and decided to wait till they got home. *If anyone calls I'll be back at four. Is Meyer in today?* (Meyer was the salesman who came in several times a week to help out, especially during the busy season.)

Not today.

All right, she said, hesitated and went out to the street, got into the car and started on her rounds for the day. But all she could really think about was Hymie.

******

Back at the bar Hymie was going through the day in a daze. There was plenty of time, after all. Four months, to be exact, and Adam was there to help him. He watched the angel out of the corner of his eye. His...what was he...his guardian seemed to have not a care in the world. He was busy spreading happiness and joy among the patrons of Fifty Bar and Grill. That was all well and good. But what about the proprietor of Fifty Bar and Grill? What was to become of him? Business had never been so good, and this depressed Hymie even more, because he was sure that he would not be around to enjoy the profits. By closing time Hymie was exhausted. He was, after all, still recovering from a near fatal illness. In addition to that the mental anxiety was draining him. Phil left early and finally the two of them were alone, the doomed mortal and his personal angel.

You look tired, Hymie. said Adam. *You worried?*

Why should I be worried? I've got an angel working for me. Tell me something.

What?

If you were in my place...?

I couldn't be.

Why not?

Because I've always been an angel.

(Interesting.) *What should I do?*

You've got to find a substitute.

Or what?

Or die.

Just like that.

It happens every day.

Not to me it doesn't. I mean it's just once, you know and that's it.

That's true.

I'm not afraid of dying. It's just that...

Your family.

What's to become of them?

When you're dead your responsibility ends.

Hymie looked searchingly at the angel. *How important are you?*

At the moment, not very, I'm afraid, said Adam and he set about cleaning up. He worked as if he'd spent all his life in the bar, all of his present existence, that is. *I'll clean up, Hymie. You can go home, if you like.*

If I like, thought Hymie. If I like. He gazed out the window of Fifty Bar and Grill. The empty street. The street light on the corner. The darkened houses across the way. People were asleep in there without a care. Their lives lay ahead of them. But did it? The Angel of Death was out there somewhere. Who knew whom the man in the black suit with the goatee would tap on the shoulder and say, "Come with me, my friend."? It happened every minute, Adam had said. And so it did. What was the point of it all? Jack, Frieda's brother, said there was no point. We were born to suffer and die and Jack was an educated man. A little obnoxious, perhaps, full of hot air, perhaps, but he was a scholar. He'd even spent some time in Palestine. Well, at least Hymie wasn't as miserable as Jack. That was some consolation. Or was it? If one were truly miserable then death might be welcome. And then he thought of Molly, Jack's wife and Jack's little boy. No. It might be all right to be miserable, but to make other people miserable? Was that fair? The phone brought Hymie out of his reverie.

Hello? he said as he picked up the receiver.

Is that you? Frieda asked.

What's the matter?

How are you feeling?

I'm feeling fine. I'll be home soon.

Tillie wants you to call her.

Tonight?

No, no. In the morning.

What does she want?

I don't know.

Did you tell her?

She asked me, so I told her.

All right, all right. I'll see you soon, he said and hung up.

Tillie was sure to be full of all sorts of advice. She was always telling everybody what to do. Poor patient Morris with his crippled leg. Well, at least Frieda didn't insult him in public the way Tillie did Morris. There'd been no other woman for him but Frieda and, though Frieda had her daydreams, he was sure she felt the same. Or did their marriage seem so rosy because it might not last for very much longer? And suppose he was gone? Who would want to marry a woman with two children, even though she was an attractive woman? After the funeral expenses, what would be left? What would become of her? What would become of the children?

Wake up, old boy!

It was Adam. Hymie looked about. He was still standing by the phone, the receiver in his hand. Ever since his illness the world seemed to be moving in slow motion. He put on his jacket, bid Adam good night and left the bar. He got into the car and he just sat there. He was immobilized by the myriad questions that crowded his brain. To be presented with ones' own death at the age of forty. How was one to deal with that? Maybe Frieda would have some ideas. She was, after all, an intelligent woman. A bit hysterical at times, but practical. And the situation called for practicality. No emotion. No regrets. Clear thinking. He was still alive and he would continue to be, all things being normal. Normal! Hah! If I keep up like this, he said to himself, I'll worry myself to death before winter comes, and he started the car. He drove slowly and carefully even though he was perfectly sober and, before he knew it, he was home. The light was on in the kitchen. Frieda was waiting up for him. They kissed, and Frieda was different somehow. She was more like she'd been before the children came. Could they be lovers again the way they used to be? Three months of that and maybe he'd be ready to face that man in the black suit with the goatee.

Would you like something to eat? she asked.

Hymie shook his head.

Are you still sick?

No. What did Tillie have to say?

She'll think of something.

What?

I don't know.

You told her everything?

You know Tillie. Maybe we should have a talk with her. You do need a pair of pants. She said she'd be in the store around noon. We don't have to stay long.

I should be in the place by twelve.

So you'll be there twelve thirty. Adam's there, isn't he?

Obviously the two women had something in mind. What the hell! Maybe they'd come up with something. After all Tillie was a fantastic business woman. Hymie and Frieda sat at the kitchen table and the talk turned to commonplace things...the house, the children, the relatives. Everything except the issue foremost in their minds. Finally Frieda went into the bedroom and waited while Hymie got ready for bed. That night...it was morning, really...for the first time in weeks they made love.

CHAPTER FOUR

TILLIE

He has to be in the place by half past twelve. All right, so we'll see you around eleven o'clock. No, no. I didn't say anything.

Hymie lay in bed half asleep, half awake, half listening to the whispered conversation Frieda was having with Tillie on the phone. It was nice to luxuriate between the clean sheets. He opened his eyes and looked dreamily at the drawn eggshell colored window shades, at the mirror on the wall over the dressing table, at the partially closed bedroom door slightly ajar. He thought he had heard the children leave for school some time ago. This was Frieda's domain just as Fifty Bar and Grill was his. What would this apartment be like when he was gone? What would happen to Fifty Bar and Grill when he was no longer there to run it? But his mind refused to answer these questions. He was alive. He was healthy and he was in the prime of life. Frieda's body floated before his eyes and the memory of their lovemaking warmed his entire being. He stretched, made waking noises and turned on his side. He should call "the place" and find out what was going on. Well, Adam was there and certainly one of God's assistants could keep an eye on a simple bar. I am certainly not going to die, he said to himself. Not this winter at any rate. The sun is shining. I can smell the fresh air. My heart is beating regularly. If one is to die one has to have some sort or premonition, some sort of warning. When his father died, he was seriously ill for quite some time.

Nu? What are you thinking?

Frieda stood at the far side of the bed. Hymie held out his hand to her.

It's time to get up, she said.

I'd better call "the place".

I called already. Adam said not to worry. Everything's under control.

I'd better talk to him anyway.

He got into his slippers, came around the bed and took Frieda into his arms. *It's almost ten o'clock,* she said.

What happens at ten o'clock?

In another hour it'll be eleven o'clock, and that's when Tillie's expecting us, said Frieda.

45

The world, the world. There really was no time to live. He kissed Frieda gently and went into the bathroom. The sun was everywhere. It flooded the house. It reflected on the white basin and the mirror so that Hymie could barely see to shave. How beautiful Frieda looked this morning. The little wrinkles around the corners of her eyes, the little lines around her mouth made her even more attractive. He wasn't that bad himself. He eyed his face critically in the mirror and was quite pleased with what he saw. He was beginning to get a little double chin, and his hair was a little thinner perhaps but aside from that (and the bags under his eyes which had always been there anyway) he was not bad looking. The image of the hollow skull that popped into his head was pushed aside. He'd never been plagued by morbid thoughts before. Was he getting to be just like his wife, full of all sorts of phobias? Perhaps he ought to take Frieda's "nerves" more seriously. He came into the kitchen to find his breakfast on the table and Frieda all ready to go, except for the apron around her waist. *You're not gonna rush me?* he said.

You're the one that wanted to be back by twelve.

I took the morning off and I'm going to enjoy it.

Who's stopping you? she said.

Fuss, fuss, fuss, fuss, fuss. He ate his breakfast slowly, watching Frieda out of the corner of his eye getting edgier and edgier.

What about the children? he asked.

Their lunch is all ready. Mrs. Newman said she'd come downstairs and make sure they ate everything.

He gulped down the last spoon of oatmeal and shoved the bowl aside. *There,* he said. *Are you satisfied?*

Some of it's still on your mouth.

Hymie wiped his mouth with his fingers.

Now go wash your hands, came the next order.

Hymie shook his head, went into the bathroom and washed his hands. When the man in the black suit with the goatee came for Frieda he'd better watch out. Come to think of it, Frieda herself would probably summon the Angel of Death when she was good and ready, and not before. Hymie looked forward to seeing Tillie. He was fond of her, though he did resent the fact that she treated him like a child. It's true she was his older sister, but he was a married man now, and a father as well. What was it about Jewish women? Always bossing their men around. Well, not in this house! *I'm ready,* he said, smiling brightly.

Get the car out. I'll meet you in front.

Had he put the car in the garage last night? Yes, he had. Strange day. One minute it was cloudy. The next minute the sun was out. Frieda stood in front of the house, waiting for him.

Have you got enough gas? she asked.

Plenty. Is that a new dress?

She looked at him in disgust. *It's three years old.*

I never saw it before.

You never looked.

So much for the amenities.

If you need a new dress, why don't you buy one?

If you'll give me the money, I'll buy one.

He took a five dollar bill from his pocket and handed it to her.

Thank you, she said and put the bill into her pocketbook.

You gonna buy a dress? he asked.

With this I can buy the sleeves.

Money, money, money. That's all that seemed to matter. Well, come December that would all be over with. They rode in silence.

Hymie, please!

What? What's the matter?

You almost hit that car.

I had the right of way.

So that's what they'll put on your tombstone.

The words were out of her mouth, too late to regret them. She sat watching him as he drove. What a strange creature her husband was! At times he could be terribly attractive, and at other times he could be so ugly. Were all men like that? She loved him, she guessed. What difference did it make? He was her fate and, I suppose, vice versa. And then she began to worry. Not about the children, for a change. She began to worry about this man...her husband, her lover, her partner. She had neglected him, but the fault wasn't hers. She had just so much to give and the children drained her dry. But she had never neglected his physical needs. Her conscience was clear in that area. He'd always been well fed, well clothed and reasonably satisfied in all such areas, she hoped. One had ones duties to fulfill, and that's what life was all about.

We're going to have to get a new car, he said.

What's wrong with this one?

It's ten years old.

So? It works, doesn't it?

When it stops working, it'll be too late.

The closer they got to Tillie and Morris' store the more uneasy Hymie became. Tillie was a bit of a bully, and it wasn't as if he were coming to Tillie for some business advice, or to borrow some money, God forbid. This was literally a matter of life and death. Usually Hymie enjoyed this trip through the alien streets, but this time his mind was plagued with doubts and apprehension.

Orange, New Jersey was where Tillie and Morris had their clothing store, and East Orange was where they lived. There weren't many Jews in the Oranges, and even the houses along the streets had a rather cold and formal appearance. Neat and unlived in.

As they drove along Main Street they passed the Palace Theatre and Frieda noticed that the film with Charles Boyer was playing there, too. She wondered when it would be coming to Hawthorne Avenue. A fine time to think about movies. She might be losing her husband and all she could think about was Charles Boyer. She looked forward to seeing her sister-in-law. Tillie had such a zest for life and it was contagious. And besides, she was anxious to share this unbearable dilemma with someone. There was the little park in the center of Main Street with that awful looking cannon, some sort of a war memorial. How she hated even the very thought of war! They were approaching the clothing store. Not that she really expected Tillie to be of much help, but you never knew. Hymie found a parking space a few doors away from the store, parked the car and they got out. There it was. KAUFMAN. MEN'S CLOTHING. They stopped and looked in the window.

That's a nice suit, said Frieda.

Hymie shrugged.

You need a new suit, she said. *Bertha's getting married in January*.

Who's Bertha?

Bertha Bender. Sol's sister. We were invited.

That means we have to get a present

Even if we don't go we'll have to get a present, she said and entered the store.

Hymie followed her in. Morris was waiting on a customer. He excused himself and limped over. He kissed Frieda and shook hands with Hymie. *Come in, come in*, he said. *It's good to see you. Tillie's in the back. She's waiting for you. Go inside. I'll be with you in a minute*, and he limped back to his customer. *This is a good suit. Look at the material. Look at the workmanship. I wouldn't sell you a piece of garbage. You can get a cheaper suit down the block, if that's what you're looking for and you'll save a few pennies. But this is a suit you'll wear for years. It's not a piece of tissue paper. Here. Let me try this jacket on you.*

Hymie followed Frieda to the back of the store. She stopped short. *This is a nice suit*, she said.

I'm not gonna buy a suit.

You need one.

Hymie was tempted to say, I may be dead in January, but he said nothing. Frieda took the hint and moved on.

Now listen, Captain Anderson, eventually you know you're going to join my suit club. Every fire house in the Oranges is in my books and now I'm starting on you policemen. And you know when I start on something, that's it. What's that? Cut the jokes. I'm serious. I want your business. (Tillie was on the phone.) *Look, I'm paying you a compliment. I always start at the top. If I get you to join I know all the others will follow, because that's how important you are. It may be a lot of crap, but it happens to be true. The trouble with you is you don't know how important you are. I was talking to Senator Chase just the other day, and he said to me, "Tillie, if I had your knowledge of psychology I'd be running for president." So I'm not talking off the top of my head.* (Tillie saw Hymie and Frieda and waved to them without missing a beat.) *Now look, Captain Anderson, in your position you've got to dress well. There you go, running yourself down again. I want to see you. No, I don't just drop by. I make an appointment. When are you free? What time? All right, I'm writing that down in my appointment book. Tomorrow afternoon at three o'clock sharp. I'll be there and you better be there, too. I don't want the run-around. You sign up with my suit club and I'll show you how sweet I can be. Okay, Captain Anderson. Tomorrow at three,* and she hung up. *Son-of-a-bitch! He's been giving me the run around for months.* She kissed Frieda and then Hymie. *How are you feeling?* she asked.

Hymie shrugged.

What is that supposed to mean? she asked.

All right.

All right? That's an answer? All right?

He's much better, Frieda said.

I don't know why you can't speak like a human being. When you get down there in your bar with all those drunks, I'll bet you speak up.

Frieda fidgeted nervously. She wished Tillie were just a bit more diplomatic, not that she hadn't taken the words right out of her mouth.

How long have you been wearing that jacket? Tillie continued.

A few months.

A few years would be more like it. Pick yourself out a jacket.

I don't need a jacket.

He needs a suit, Frieda said. *Bertha Bender's getting married in January and he has nothing to wear.*

You were invited? How do you like that? They didn't even invite us, and I know Bertha as well as you.

It's gonna be a very small wedding.

I don't take up that much room. That's all right. I won't even send them a card. Out of sight, out of mind. We went to school together. Excuse me one minute. I gotta make one more call and I'll be right with you.

Go ahead, Frieda said and Tillie went back to the phone. *Why don't you try on a suit?* Frieda urged.

Frija, I'm not gonna buy a suit.

You don't have to get it now. Just try it on, that's all.

What's the use of trying it on if I'm not gonna buy it?

Do me a favor. I've never seen such a stubborn man. We're not that poor. You need a suit. You can't go to the wedding in that jacket you're wearing.

What's the matter? asked Tillie as she rejoined them.

I want him to try on a suit.

I'm not gonna get a suit.

Come with me, Tillie ordered.

I don't want a suit.

Shut up and come with me!

Not wishing to make a scene Hymie followed his sister to a rack full of suits. She took a suit jacket from its hanger and handed it to Hymie. *Try that on. Try it on!*

Hymie obeyed. It was too tight.

You're getting fat, Tillie snapped and returned the jacket to the hanger. She moved down the rack. *Try this one.*

Tillie, I'm not...

Try it on!

Hymie obeyed.

That's a little better, said Tillie.

The color's not bad, said Frieda.

Turn around, Tillie barked. *It doesn't fit. We're getting in more stuff next week. Let's wait and see what we get. Now let's find you a pair of pants. What color do you want?*

Brown, said Frieda. *Dark brown.*

How fat have you gotten? asked Tillie as she picked up a tape measure.

I haven't gotten fat. Hymie protested.

Tillie measured Hymie's waist and picked out a pair of trousers. *You're beginning to get a pot. Here, try these. Go in the back.*

Hymie put on the trousers and returned to the front of the store.

I think they're a little too tight, said Frieda.

Tillie put the trousers back on the hanger. *You don't want a check, do you? How about a nice gray?*

Maybe a pair of black or navy blue, said Frieda.

Here, try these, said Tillie and she handed him a pair of dark gray trousers. *Go in the back and try them on.*

Hymie hesitated.

What's the matter now? said Tillie.

Hymie took the trousers, went to the back of the store. He hated this whole ridiculous ritual. Whenever they came here they never got exactly what they wanted and, though Tillie did charge them cost price, he often thought they could save more money by going to any department store. They had decided on brown or Frieda had, at any rate, and here he was, getting into a pair of gray. Well, pants are pants, he said to himself, zipped up the fly and came out into the front of the store.

They're fine, said Tillie with finality.

You like them? asked Frieda.

What's not to like? said Tillie.

They're nice, said Frieda. *You like them?*

You're not gonna wear them to the wedding, are you? said Tillie.

That's a good pair of pants, said Morris as he joined them.

What did he want? Tillie asked Morris, referring to the customer who had just gone out the door.

Nothing. Absolutely nothing. I waste more time.

Did you mention the suit club?

He's a bum. Suit club!

Everybody's a bum by you. You're the bum.

You haven't bought a suit in a long time, Hymie. We just got in some suits, said Morris.

There's nothing for him.

How about...?

I said there's nothing for him. Are you deaf or something?

I just thought...

If you sold more clothes and did less thinking I wouldn't have to run myself ragged getting people to join the suit club.

You and your suit club. You think that's the answer to the problems of the world.

If it wasn't for my suit club you wouldn't have had any breakfast this morning. Will you do me a favor, please, and measure those cuffs for my brother instead of arguing with me?

You want those pants? Morris asked.

Of course he wants the pants. That's what he came here for. Does he want the pants?!

Do you want them? Frieda asked.

I don't know, said Hymie. *What do you think?*

I'm surrounded by idiots, groaned Tillie. *Will you please take him in the back and measure him for those cuffs, for God sakes! He's getting a pair of pants, not a wedding dress.*

So take them, said Frieda.

Tillie sighed in disgust. Morris took Hymie to the back of the store and measured the cuffs. *That's a nice pair of pants you're getting,* he said. *You need them right away?*

No.

I'll have them by the end of the week. If you want you can pick them up on Friday, or we can bring them over with us on Sunday.

You're coming over Sunday?

How are you feeling?

Much better.

How's business?

What's the use of complaining?

Hymie hadn't meant to say that. He'd wanted to say that business was pretty good. But there he was, assuming Frieda's negative attitude.

Okay, you can take them off.

Hymie went behind the screen, took off the new trousers and put on his old ones.

I'm sure you have nothing to worry about, said Morris.

Did the whole world know about his predicament? Well, maybe it was for the best. If enough people knew maybe some madman would come forward and volunteer to take his place. Morris, for example. What fun did he get out of life? On the one hand (on the one leg) he was crippled. He could barely get about. On the other, he was continually subjected to Tillie's derision.

I'll wait for you out front, said Morris.

When Hymie came out from behind the screen he was confronted by Tillie. *Sit down. I want to talk to you*, she said.

Hymie sat down and Tillie sat next to him.

I want you to start from the beginning and tell me everything.

Hymie did as he was told and, to his amazement, Tillie listened attentively without interrupting him once. When he was finished the questions began.

How old is this Adam?

He could be thirty. He could be forty. He could be twenty five. He's a young man. A young angel.

He looks young.

And you have until when?

Till winter

December twenty-first?

Four months.

I want to meet him.

Who?

Who?! This Adam. I wanna have a talk with him.

Hymie looked uneasy.

What's the matter? she continued.

There's nothing more he can do. He told me so.

I've never been face to face with an angel.

Tillie, he doesn't need a suit.

Hymie, do me a favor. All right?

All right, all right, so you'll meet him.

I want you to invite him to dinner.

Where?

To your house. It's all right. I spoke to Frija and she'd be only too happy to have him.

So that was it. They were going to butter Adam up with a good meal and then Tillie would go to work on him. What a waste of time! But what choice did he have? He couldn't afford to turn his nose up at any alternative.

All right, I'll ask him. When?

Sunday afternoon. This Sunday. We'll be there around two.

Hymie sighed and nodded.

Don't worry. Everything's gonna be all right. Have I ever let you down?

Hymie was non-plussed to remember what Tillie had ever really done for him. Well, she did feed him home cooked meals when he first came to America, before Frieda had come over to join him. *All right, I'll ask him.*

Tillie rose. *And do me a favor, don't drink so much. And take it easy. If this Adam is helping out in "the place" you can afford to take a little time off. It's over before you know it. So enjoy yourself a little.*

That had an ominous note. Tillie wasn't as sure of her powers as she would like him to believe.

So what did you and Tillie talk about? asked Frieda on the way home.

Hymie played along. *She wants us to invite Adam to dinner on Sunday.*

So what did you tell her?

I told her I would.

They drove the rest of the way home in silence. By the time Hymie got back to the bar the noon rush was almost over. *You got a couple of calls this morning*, said Phil. *I wrote them down.* Hymie looked at the pad near the phone. A salesman. The insurance man. The accountant. Nothing pressing. He glanced over at Adam, tending bar. The angel didn't seem to be as bright and as cheerful as usual. Hymie caught his eye. *Can I speak to you for a minute?* said Hymie.

Sure, said Adam and followed Hymie into the kitchen.

Phil eyed them suspiciously.

My wife said to bring you home for dinner on Sunday.

Fine.

Everything all right?

No answer.

Is there anything wrong?

I don't like it here, the angel said finally. *Oh, I don't mean here in the bar. I mean here, on earth. I guess I'm just homesick.*

I'm sorry to hear that.

Have you made any progress?

Hymie looked blank.

In your search for a substitute?

No. Not yet. So we'll see you on Sunday then. I'll be down in the morning to pick you up.

The phone rang and Phil answered it.

It's your wife, Hymie.

Hymie excused himself and went to the phone. *What is it?*

Have you asked him?

Yes.

Is he coming.

Yes. Why?

I thought maybe there was something special I could make that he would like.

Hymie glanced over at Adam, then cupped his hand around the phone and spoke so as not to be overheard. *He's an angel. What does he know about cooking? Whatever you make, he'll eat.*

If you get a chance, find out what he likes.

All right, all right. Is there anything else?

No. And she hung up.

Hymie hung up and rejoined Adam in the kitchen. *That was my wife. She was wondering if there was anything special you'd like to eat.*

I can't think of anything.

She'll probably make roast chicken or roast beef. She's a very good cook.

Sounds fine to me. Do you mind if I take off for a couple of hours?

Hymie tried to hide his surprise. *No. No, of course not.*

I'd just like to take a walk.

Go ahead.

Adam took off his apron, hung it up and walked out through the swinging doors. Hymie watched him apprehensively. His private angel was showing signs of wear and tear. That was not a good sign.

CHAPTER FIVE

SUNDAY DINNER

Sunday started out to be a miserable day. Early in the morning it rained and thundered and after that the sky remained overcast. Hymie usually slept later on Sundays and this morning he slept even later than usual. (He was finding it harder and harder to get up in the morning.) The house was full of all sorts of exotic smells...herbs and garlic. Frieda was in the kitchen busier than ever. Pots and pans were everywhere. *You've got to get me some rolls and some bread*, she said

I've got to pick Adam up. I'll get them on the way back.

By that time there'll be nothing left. Please, Hymie, don't give me an argument. Not this morning. If I live through today... She stopped herself and wiped her forehead with her apron. She really had to watch her tongue. *Look at me. I'm soaked through and through.*

All right. I'll get the bread. Can I have some breakfast first?

You'll have to help yourself. I've got a million things to do. All right, all right. Sit down. I've been up since six o'clock this morning.

So who told you to get up so early?

Please, Hymie. Do you know what it takes to cook a dinner? I started on Wednesday and I haven't stopped. There's your coffee. You don't need any cereal this morning. Eat some bread.

What about my juice?

Get it yourself.

Hymie poured himself some orange juice, sat at the kitchen table and ate his breakfast. Frieda went back to her pots and pans. *What were you dreaming?* she asked.

Dreaming?

You kept saying, "Fill 'er up. Fill 'er up."

I don't know.

Hymie was convinced she was making up all these stories about his snoring and talking in his sleep, and the tossing and the turning. Of course, he did have something to toss turn about now.

Take the children with you to the bakery, she said.

Hymie lit a cigarette and smoked while he drank his coffee.

A cigarette already? You just got up.

Hymie coughed.

Have another puff, she said.

Hymie looked about. Despite all the clutter it all seemed so calm and serene this Sunday morning. Outside the rain was coming down again. And here in the kitchen Frieda was busy making dinner and complaining as usual. He could hear the children's voices in the front room. Rachel's voice, high and piping. Nathan's, calm and superior. Hymie finished his coffee, rose from the kitchen table and started towards the front of the house.

And please don't used the floor as an ash tray. I just cleaned up in there.

Hymie put out the cigarette in a nearby ash tray and walked through the dining room into the living room. Rachel was on the floor working on a coloring book. Nathan lay sprawled on the sofa, reading. It was hard to believe that he and Frieda had spawned these two human beings.

Daddy, Daddy, Daddy! Rachel jumped up from the floor and threw her arms around his waist. Hymie lifted the girl in his arms and she kissed him. He kissed her back, marveling at her creamy complexion, her bright shining eyes, her lustrous curls. And she was getting heavy, too. *What are you doing?* Hymie asked.

I'm working on my coloring book.

Mother said we could go to the bakery with you, Nathan said from the sofa.

Mommy said we could pick our own cupcakes, Rachel added.

Good. Let's go, said Hymie as he put the girl down.

Take the umbrella, Frieda shouted from the kitchen.

We don't need an umbrella, replied Nathan. *It's not raining that hard.*

I said, take an umbrella.

Nathan ran out the front door and onto the porch.

Hymie, take an umbrella.

I'll get it, I'll get it, chirped Rachel and ran through the kitchen to the coat stand in the back foyer. *It isn't here.*

It's in the front closet, said Frieda.

Rachel ran into the front closet and came out with a large man's umbrella which she handed to Hymie. *Here, Daddy.*

Get a rye bread with seeds. Sliced. Not too brown.

A large or a small one? asked Hymie.

Make it a small one. I've still got some left. No, make it a large one. Tillie might wanna take some home. And a dozen rolls. Make sure they're not burnt. Half with seeds, half without.

And our cupcakes, Mommy.

And a half a dozen cupcakes. Let them pick them out.

You need anything else? he asked.

Another pair of hands.

Hymie and Rachel started out.

Get a couple of quarts of milk. Just in case they decide to stay for supper. You hear me?

Yes. Yes, I hear you.

It's really not raining that hard, said Nathan as Hymie and Rachel came onto the porch. *I'll hold the umbrella for you.*

Let me, let me, piped Rachel.

You're too small, said Nathan.

Hymie handed the umbrella to Nathan who opened it and held it over the three of them as they walked down the stairs to the car.

I'm getting wet. I'm getting wet, cried Rachel.

It'll make you grow, said Nathan.

When they had finally settled into the car and were ready to leave, Frieda came running out onto the porch. *Hymie! Hymie, get some pickles and some sauerkraut. You hear me?*

I hear you, I hear you.

Four pickles and a pound of sauerkraut, Frieda added.

They drove off, the children waving at Frieda. It was a short drive to the bakery...down half a block to Goodwin Avenue, left three blocks to Hawthorne Avenue and up Hawthorne Avenue three and a half blocks, just above Clinton Place. It took a few minutes to find a parking place. Hymie held the umbrella over the three of them as they walked from the car to the store. The children made a game of hopping over the puddles. Despite the rain Silvers' bakery was packed. Nathan took a numbered ticket from the little machine on the counter and handed it to Hymie and they waited their turn. Hymie waited on the side of the store where the bread and rolls were kept. The children ran over to the other side and gazed wide-eyed at all the cakes and cookies. Hymie studied his offsprings as they moved about the store. Nathan was a bright, nice looking boy, sensitive and spoiled. He would probably be a doctor or a lawyer or a teacher, that is if they could afford to send him to college. Frieda had great ambition for her son and Hymie knew that if she had anything to say about it, and she most certainly did, Nathan would undoubtedly attend college. He was his mother's son and Hymie knew of no way he could retrieve the ground he had lost. How does one communicate with ones own flesh and blood who was not really ones own somehow? What did they have in common? They shared Frieda. They shared the same house and that was about it. Hymie was not an educated man. He was not a native American, and when did he have the time to sit down and talk to the boy? And what would they talk about anyway? Nathan was not into baseball.

Number forty six, the sales girl called.

That's me, said Hymie and he handed her the ticket and purchased the bread and the rolls.

Daddy, daddy! called Rachel. *Don't forget the cupcakes.*

Hymie moved to the other counter and, after much debate, the cupcakes were finally purchased. Three with strawberry icing, two with chocolate and one vanilla. Hymie bought each of the children a cookie to eat there and then, warning them not to tell their mother because Frieda would scold and say that it would spoil their appetite. When they came out of the bakery the rain had stopped and there was no need for the umbrella. Nathan carried the bag of bread and rolls and Rachel carried the little white box with the cupcakes. They were halfway to the car when Hymie remembered the milk and he sent Nathan back to the dairy store next to the bakery. They stopped at Tabatchnicks for the pickles and sauerkraut, then headed home.

What took you so long? asked Frieda as them came through the doorway.

We had to stand in line, said Nathan.

Tillie just called. They'll be here at two. What time are you gonna pick up Adam?

I thought I'd go down now.

Can we go, too? asked Rachel.

I need you here, said Frieda. *Nathan, will you please take out the garbage? I asked you fifty times already. Then you and Rachel can set the table.*

Could this establishment function without him? Hymie wondered. Quite possibly, if it had to. *I'm going,* he said to Frieda.

So go already. By time you get down there and back it'll be two o'clock already.

Hymie hesitated. He would have liked to take the children with him, but he didn't want to make an issue of it. And besides, he knew that Frieda wasn't too keen about Nathan spending any time around the bar.

I thought you were going.

I'm going, I'm going.

You didn't change your shirt? Frieda asked. *Hymie, please, do me a favor and change your shirt.*

What shirt shall I wear?

A clean one. She went to the bureau in the corner of the dining room next to the closet, took a neatly ironed shirt from the drawer and handed it to him. *Is that the only tie you have?*

What's wrong with this tie?

It has a spot on it. Here. Wear this one. What are you saving it for? And she took a tie from a box and handed it to Hymie. Hymie had forgotten he had it.

This suit doesn't look too bad, Hymie said, looking for her approval. Frieda shrugged noncommittally and went back to work. *The dinner will be ready soon and nobody will be here,* she muttered.

Hymie went into the bathroom to change his shirt and tie then inspected himself in the mirror. Very elegant. And there was certainly nothing wrong with the suit. So it was a little shiny here and there. Who noticed? It still fitted him.

Did you put the dirty shirt in the hamper? Frieda asked.

Yes, I put the shirt in the hamper.

Now you look like a "mensch".

(Good lord! Was that a compliment?)

What did you do with the tie?

It's in the bathroom. Shall I hang it up?

You have a tie rack, don't you? That's what I bought it for.

Hymie went back into the bathroom, took the tie from the door knob and hung it on the tie rack on the back of the closet door in the bedroom. *So, I'm going,* he said. *Did you hear me?*

I thought you were gone already.

Damn her self-sufficiency, Hymie thought as he left the house. Then again, maybe he wasn't being fair to her. Other husbands did spend more time with their wives. But he was in the saloon business, early in the morning till late at night. It was the only business he knew. It was too late to try something else. Then again, maybe not. If he did survive this dilemma he would find another business. Why not?! He was still a young man. Why shouldn't he have a social life, just like other men? But all these mundane matters sank to nothingness when he thought about his dilemma. He wondered what Jack would have to say about it. Frieda's brother had an answer for everything. Maybe he ought to call him. No, that wouldn't do. This wasn't something for a phone conversation.

They'd have to pay him a visit. Next Sunday maybe. Next Sunday they would pay Jack and Molly a visit.

Every once in a while the sun broke through the clouds. What a strange day! The sun, the rain, the clouds all at once. And the stronger the sun the higher grew Hymie's hopes.

There were only two customers in the place when Hymie arrived. They were playing shuffleboard, the game Hymie had installed a few months ago. Frieda was very upset when she heard how much it cost. (She wormed it out of him.) Adam was behind the bar. He looked a little brighter and happier.

All ready? Hymie asked.

All ready, Adam replied.

Hymie felt a pang of pity and of guilt as he looked at his angel. Adam looked rather shabby and, to be quite frank, he was beginning to smell. It was still warm these days and Adam worked hard and, if one got close enough, his body odor was overpowering. Hymie couldn't quite figure it out. Adam didn't shave (he was positive of that.) and yet his face was as smooth as could be. He did perspire profusely though, and he certainly ate and he went to the bathroom.

Is there anything wrong? Adam asked. *My clothes are not very clean, I know. I was going to wash them out, only I was afraid that they wouldn't dry in time.*

If you don't mind, I can let you have some of mine when we get home. And, if you like, you can take a bath. Hymie hoped he had stated it diplomatically.

I guess I need one, don't I? replied the angel.

Hymie said nothing, but did some quick thinking. Adam should have some place to stay, with a bathroom that had a bathtub and a regular bedroom. The Kopanskis upstairs had an extra room they rented out from time to time and, as far as he knew, it was available. Hymie excused himself, went upstairs and knocked on Kopanski's door. Frank Kopanski, himself, in his undershirt, opened the door. *Hey, Hymie, how you doin? Come on in, come on in. How about a cup of coffee. Mary's in church or she'd make you sit down and have some breakfast.*

I really don't have time. My wife's expecting me home for dinner. We have some company coming.

Hey, that was some party the other night, wasn't it? You devil, you! You're quite a dancer. Mary said to me, "That Hymie's as graceful as a cat."

Hymie grinned foolishly. *I'm not a very good dancer.*

Not according to Mary. Hey,how about a little shot? An eye-opener? Come on. I've still got that bottle of Scotch you gave me for my birthday.

Well, maybe just a short one.

This one's on me, said Frank as he poured two healthy drinks. He sat Hymie down at the dining room table and he was off and running. Baseball, neighborhood gossip, family complaints, local politics, national politics. It was almost twenty minutes before Hymie was able to get around to discussing the room. It was available and they'd be glad to have Adam. (Hymie did not reveal Adam's true identity. After all, he was a Jewish angel and maybe he wouldn't be an angel for a goy.) Hymie put down a week's deposit and was ready to leave but Frank wouldn't hear of it. They had another drink and Hymie finally broke away, promising faithfully that he'd bring the wife and kids down for a visit some Sunday. Adam seemed pleased to hear about the room. They locked the place up, set the alarm, got into the car and drove home. (The bar was open only half a day on Sunday.) The sun was now shining brightly. Not a cloud in the sky.

The children were sitting on the porch when they pulled up in front of the house. They had spread some papers on the cement so as not to dirty their good clothes. Rachel ran down the steps to greet them. Nathan followed at a dignified distance. They seemed a little shyer with Adam this time. They didn't even offer to shake hands and Hymie wondered if they remembered their previous meeting. They had been half asleep. Adam, himself, seemed a little ill at ease.

You remember Adam, Hymie said.

Rachel nodded and Nathan offered his hand. *How do you do,* said Nathan.

How do you do, Adam replied and shook Nathan's hand. Rachel backed away.

Aren't you going to say hello to Adam? Hymie asked his daughter.

Hello.

Hello, Rachel, said the angel.

Frieda came out onto the porch, wiping her hands on her apron. *Hello*, said Frieda to Adam as he came up the stairs. *I'm glad you could come.*

It's very nice of you to ask me.

Please. Come in, come in. Adam walked through the foyer and Hymie whispered to Frieda about the clothes and the bath. Frieda frowned, sighed and turned to Adam. *My sister-in-law and her husband should be here soon,* she said. *Meanwhile, if you'd like to clean up. As a matter of fact, if you'd like to take a bath, I'm sure you'lll have time.*

That would be nice, said Adam quickly and Frieda led the angel into the bathroom.

He smells, said Rachel.

Shhhh, Hymie whispered.

Well, he does. Doesn't he take a bath?

He's an angel. Angels don't take baths, Nathan sneered.

They will today, said Hymie.

Then maybe he isn't an angel, said Nathan.

I never said he was an angel, said Hymie.

Well, is he or isn't he? Nathan asked.

What do you think? replied Hymie.

Of course, he's an angel, scoffed Rachel. *But he's in human form.*

Out of the mouths of babes. That settled that. Because Hymie had begun to have his doubts. He himself was about as human as a human could be, and if Adam was working for him, well...

Maybe you should buy him some clothes, Frieda muttered as she came into the dining room and began to ransack the bureaus drawers. *Here, give this to him,* she said and handed Hymie some underwear, a shirt and socks. Hymie knocked on the bathroom door and Adam stuck his head out. *Oh, thank you,* said Adam as he took the clothes and shut the door again.

You have two pairs of slacks you can give him. They're all mended and patched.

Are they clean?

No, they're dirty! Of course, they're clean.

Then give him.

Frieda went into their bedroom and returned with a pair of slacks which Hymie passed on to Adam. Back in the kitchen Frieda said, *You should pay him a salary.*

I can't afford two salaries.

Then let Phil go.

I got him a room with the Kopanskis.

You're paying for it?

What then?

How much?

Three dollars a week.

He could stay here. On the day bed.

Never in a million years, thought Hymie. Frieda was much too fond of the angel, and he wasn't going to ask for trouble. *I'll buy him some clothes*, he said.

You need two people in "the place"?

Yes, I need two people. Especially now, since it's gotten so busy. Frieda said nothing more and went back to spooning out the chopped liver. *It's two o'clock and your sister's not here yet.*

You were the one that invited her.

It was Tillie's idea.

But you agreed.

You think I'm doing this for myself?

If you're doing it for me, for once in your life, don't complain.

Frieda looked up in astonishment. Her eyes grew moist. *I'm sorry*, she said. *I didn't mean...* She touched Hymie's sleeve in what he assumed to be a gesture of affection and walked to the sink.

You want me to put out the liver? he asked.

Let the children do it. Go. Go sit in the front and read your paper.

Hymie went into the front room, sent the children into Frieda and sat down on the couch with the Jewish Daily Forward but he couldn't read. He got up and paced about the room. If only one could do things for oneself. If only one weren't so dependant on others. That's why the world was in such a mess. No one really communicated with one other. We're born alone and we die alone. A thought worthy of Jack, Frieda's sarcastic brother. Hymie saw the Kaufman car pull up and Tillie get out from behind the steering wheel. She waited as Morris limped to catch up with her. *They're here*, he called out.

They're here, they're here! Rachel shouted, jumping up and down. *Mommy, they're here.*

All right, all right. So they're here. Frieda came into the dining room. *Did they bring the boys?*

I don't see them, said Hymie.

They're here, they're here! Rachel chanted as she ran around the dining room table.

Why don't you calm down? Nathan admonished.

They're here, they're here! And Rachel ran to the front door and opened it.

What a child! Nathan said and followed his sister at a dignified distance.

Tillie came barreling through the door. *There she is. My favorite niece. Oh, what a darling she is. Give me a big kiss.* And she enveloped Rachel in her arms and kissed her. *Mmmmm. And we look so pretty today. Pretty as a picture.*

Hello, Aunt Tillie, Rachel murmured shyly.

Ohhh, I'm gonna eat you up. And she gave Rachel an extra hug, then went on to Nathan. *And what about my favorite nephew? Don't I get a kiss?*

Hello, Aunt Tillie.

He's too big to kiss Aunt Tillie?

No, no. Nathan mumbled, blushing, and kissed Tillie timidly.

You call that a kiss? And Tillie clasped Nathan to her amble bosom, planting a kiss on his cheek. *Now that's a kiss. And that's a kiss. And that's a kiss. You I don't have to kiss. But here's a kiss anyway.* And she kissed Hymie heartily. *And my beautiful sister-in-law.* She kissed Frieda. *Is he here?* she whispered to her. *He's in the bathroom, taking a bath.*

A bath?

There's no bathtub in "the place".

Tillie looked quizzical. *I never heard of an angel taking a bath.*

He's in human form, said Nathan.

Ah leben auf deine kopele, said Tillie and she kissed Nathan again.

Where's Herb? asked Nathan. (Herbert was the younger son.)

He was invited to a birthday party. Mmm. Something smells good. Potato Kugel. My favorite. I'm gonna gain ten pounds.

You wouldn't gain ten pounds, said Frieda. And the family greeted Morris who limped in slowly behind Tillie.

How about a drink? Hymie said to Morris.

Why not? said Morris.

Right away with the drink, said Frieda and stopped short when she saw the murderous look on Hymie's face.

Who needs a drink? said Tillie. *We'll have a drink later.*

Would you like a drink? Hymie said, ignoring the women.

Maybe later, said Morris quietly.

Well, I'm gonna have one now, said Hymie and went for the bottle.

In that case, I'll join you, said Morris.

The table looks lovely, said Tillie.

I thought you'd bring Herb, said Frieda.

He had a birthday party.

I know he likes my kugel.

So I'll bring him a piece. Let me see what you made.

No inspection. When I bring it to the table, then you'll know.

I'm starved. Don't I get a "nosh"?

Frieda couldn't resist the flattery and took Tillie into the kitchen to give her a "nosh".

Hymie came to the kitchen doorway. *Would you like a drink?*

A little sweet, said Frieda. *Maybe it'll settle my stomach.*

How about you? Hymie asked his sister.

I'll have a highball, said Tillie.

Is there any ginger ale? Hymie asked.

I think there's a bottle in the pantry, but I don't think it's cold.

So I'll drink it warm.

Put some ice in it, said Frieda.

What glasses should I use?

Take the ones from the china closet. Never mind. I'll get them. He can't wait. It's gotta be right now. Always with the drink. And she went into the dining room, took several glasses from the china closet and set them on the table for Hymie, who began to busy himself with the drinks.

Mmmm, this chicken is delicious, said Tillie in the kitchen, nibbling on a chicken wing.

I hope there's enough. I made some pot roast, just in case. said Frieda.

A very damp looking angel emerged from the bathroom in Hymie's shirt and slacks and came into the kitchen. Frieda introduced him to Tillie.

We're having a drink, said Hymie. *What would you like?*

A beer would be fine, said Adam.

Tillie looked puzzled. An angel drinking beer?

Why don't we all sit down? Everything's all ready. Frieda announced.

Can we finish our drinks? queried Hymie, a slight edge in his voice.

You can finish them at the table. I don't want everything to get cold.

Here, let me help you, said Tillie to Hymie and they carried the drinks to the table. *C'mon everybody. We're going to eat,* called Tillie.

We don't want everything to get cold. Morris, what are you doing in there?

I'm coming, I'm coming.

You sit next to me, said Tillie to Nathan then turned to Frieda. *Where shall we sit?*

Frieda was in a quandary about where to put Adam. At the head of the table? After all, an angel. But that was Hymie's place and he was there already. *Why don't you sit here, Adam*, she said to the angel, pointing to the foot of the table. *And you sit here*, she said to Tillie, placing her at Adam's left.

As long as I don't have to sit next to him, said Tillie referring to Morris. *That Russian Communist!*

Russian Communist, muttered Morris.

Well, aren't you?

Tillie, please, he protested.

Tillie, please, she mimicked. *Everyone knows it. You come from Russia and you're a Communist.*

I'm an American.

That's right, said Frieda. *You're an American and you sit here, next to Hymie.*

And the dinner began. The first appetizer was the chopped liver on a bed of lettuce, topped with a little red radish. The second appetizer was mushrooms cooked in eggs with onions. This was eaten hot over saltine crackers. Then there was a choice of chicken soup with "knedlach" or hot meat borscht with a boiled potato. (*Naturally the Communist will have the borscht*, said Tillie.) The main dish was a large, luscious brown roasted chicken with bread and mushroom stuffing and a large bowl of hot gravy to pour over it. There were sweet potatoes and boiled potatoes and potato kugel. (*Nobody can make a potato kugel like my sister-in-law*, crowed Tillie.) There were canned jellied cranberries and fresh asparagus and lima beans. There was fresh coleslaw and sauerkraut and sour pickles.

There's pot roast, if anybody wants, said Frieda.

I'm so full, said Tillie, *but I've got to taste it.*

I'm so full, said Nathan.

Me, too, said Rachel.

Have some more chicken, Adam, said Frieda.

No, thank you. I've had plenty. It's delicious.

Frieda's the best cook in New Jersey, said Tillie.

And Hymie sat proudly at the head of the table, eating heartily, despite the great burden that weighed on his mind. *If you're gonna die tomorrow, you might as well eat today.*

Just to say there was potato kugel, or just to say there was roast chicken with bread and mushroom stuffing with gravy, would be a grave injustice to Frieda, to truth and to posterity. The potato kugel was not just a potato kugel. It was a toe-curling experience, the delicacy of its flavor, the moist warmth of its texture. And the chicken! An exotic flavor unrivaled in this world and even the next, perhaps. The dessert was a noodle pudding cooked in pineapple juice.

I suppose you want coffee, said Frieda to Tillie.

If you don't mind. I'll put it up, Tillie volunteered.

Sit. It's no trouble.

The coffee, of course, was served black, since Frieda was strictly kosher. Tillie was careful to point this out to Adam. And this was an excellent springboard for Tillie to elaborate on Frieda's goodness. How religious she was, how kind, how charitable. There was always a "pishkah" to collect coins for the poor. And, of course, he knew what a good man Hymie was. Poor as they were they were always ready to share what they had with the less fortunate. And look at those children. Have you ever seen such beautiful children? So intelligent? So well behaved. It's true that Hymie was her brother, but still she had to say it. You couldn't find a finer man.

Let's open up the window and throw out the dishes, said Frieda entering from the kitchen with the coffee.

I'd like you to come to the store and pick out a nice suit, said Tillie to Adam. *Hymie, I want you to bring Adam to the store and let him pick out a suit. We're getting in a new shipment this week and you'll find something nice.*

We have an excellent tailor who does our work for us, added Morris.

Hymie's pants! They're in the car, said Tillie.

I'll get them, volunteered Nathan.

Morris gave the boy the keys to the car and Nathan left to get his father's trousers.

Have you ever seen such a beautiful boy? said Tillie to Adam.

Adam smiled politely. *They're both beautiful children,* said Adam.

And Rachel is my favorite niece, added Tillie, giving the girl a hug. Then she turned to Frieda who was beginning to clear the table. *Let me help you*, she said.

No, no. said Frieda. *The children will help. You're a guest.*

Good, said Tillie. *Because I want to have a talk with Adam. Why don't we take a walk around the block?*

All right, said Adam, rising from the table a little apprehensively. This woman was rather intimidating.

I'll make a stop first, said Tillie and headed for the bathroom.

That was an excellent meal, said Adam to Frieda.

Frieda's the best, said Morris. *There's no doubt about that.*

You want me to help you? Hymie asked Frieda.

(The world was coming to an end!) *No, no. You take Morris and go in front.*

Do I look good enough to walk with an angel? asked Tillie as she reentered the dining room patting her hair. This was the first mention she'd made of Adam's supernatural identity.

You look fine, said Adam gallantly.

Then let's go, said Tillie, slipping her hand into the crook of Adam's arm. She winked at Hymie as they walked out the front door.

She had absolutely no idea of what she was going to say or how she was going to approach this rather docile, pleasant creature. Strong arm tactics would never work. That was clear. Adam smiled at her. Could he read her mind? Was she that obvious?

You're a remarkable woman, said Adam.

What did that mean? What did he know about her?

They strolled down Nye Avenue in silence. They turned right on Goodwin Avenue for no apparent reason. Who was leading whom? They seemed be walking effortlessly and to her amazement Tillie began to feel very comfortable with this person. How peaceful, she thought. Is this what it was like in heaven? If so, why struggle? Tillie felt like a child again. No worries. No cares. Not that her childhood had been carefree. Far from it. But there had been days she remembered back on the farm...lazy days, enchanted sunny afternoons.

So what do you think of us? She surprised both Adam and herself with that question.

In what way?

Are we foolish, stupid people? Should we be ashamed of ourselves?

Why?

I don't know.

It's not your fault.

What?

Life is a gift. And just when you grow wise enough to enjoy it, it's taken away from you.

I suppose there must be a reason for it.

That doesn't make it right.

And there's nothing you can do about it?

"Gather ye rosebuds while ye may."

That's it?

I'm afraid so.

And afterwards?

I'd rather not go into that.

Why not?

Do you understand the moon and the stars and the earth? How they all came to be?

If you explain it to me.

I couldn't do that.

Why not?

If you knew everything we'd be out of a job, for one thing. And besides you're really not equipped to understand. Please don't be offended.

I'm not offended. But tell me this. Can you predict the future?

No. What kind of an angel am I, you're thinking. I'll tell you. I'm a troublemaker. That's why I'm here right now. I'm not afraid of speaking out, especially when I come across injustice.

But you can't do anything about it.

Not very much, I'm afraid. But that doesn't stop me. When I'm recalled I'll probably be called on the carpet, so to speak, for helping Hymie out. And you might as well know right now, I've done all that I can for your brother.

Tillie's heart sank. Surely there must be something she could say, something she could ask. But Adam's statement sounded so final that she decided to drop the subject...for now. This might be the closest I'll ever get to God, she thought, so maybe I'd better tread very carefully.

Does it get any easier, I wonder. I mean, there are times, when I'm alone and I sit and I ask myself, How can I go on? It's too much for one woman.

And what's the answer?

They need me. The boys, my husband. And now my brother. Maybe I'll get my reward in heaven.

Don't count on it. No, my dear, you'll get your reward right here...in the faces of your loved ones. You've accomplished so much. Take the time to be proud of that.

And now my husband may need an operation. Where will the money come from? And we don't even know if it will help. He's had two already.

What does the doctor say?

I don't know. He has an appointment this week. I don't know why I'm telling you all this.

Maybe because I'm interested. After all I am an angel and angels are caring creatures.

How many are there? Like you, I mean?

Like me? None. Look at that house. Isn't that interesting! And those flowers. Aren't they beautiful?!

Very pretty.

But you're not looking, Tillie. Stop and smell the roses.

They had reached Osborne Terrace, a lovely tree lined street with well cared for lawns and houses.

Look at all this, Adam continued. *We have nothing like this up there.*

Tillie looked confused. Adam laughed and kissed Tillie gently on the cheek. For the first time, in a very long, long time, Tillie felt that she was not in charge. It was as if a great weight had been lifted from her shoulders. Kissed by an angel! How many people can say that? Kissed by an angel! Adam was saying something.

Maybe we'd better start back. Come along.

Adam took her arm. They started back to the house and, as they walked, Tillie noticed that the leaves were beginning to change color. She saw one leaf fall slowly to the ground.

*****

Back at the house Hymie and Morris were sitting in the front room. Hymie had stood at the window watching Tillie and Adam disappear down the block.

If anyone can do anything, you can depend on Tillie, said Morris.

I don't think anybody can.

If he's really an angel, why can't he help you?

He's in disgrace.

What did he do?

I don't know.

Did you ask?

If he wants to tell me, he'll tell me. Hymie didn't feel that he could reveal the little he did know about Adam's misdeeds. He was not a gossip.

That's where you make your mistake, Hymie. You've got to take an interest in people.

He's not a person. He's an angel.

He must have been a person once, don't you think?

I don't know. But I think there were angels before there were people. Not that I remember my "chumish".

I don't suppose you'd like to hear the baseball game.

This radio doesn't work. We listen to the one in the kitchen.

I'd just like to hear the score. Do you mind?

I'll bring it in.

No, no. I'll just go into the kitchen for a minute. I'll be right back. And Morris limped into the kitchen, leaving Hymie with his anxiety.

This called for a drink. Thank God the liquor was kept in the dining room. Just as he was downing a second healthy shot Frieda came into the dining room to finish clearing the table. She made no comment about the liquor and went about her business.

I think they liked the dinner, said Hymie a little defensively. Frieda said nothing and returned to the kitchen with the salt and pepper shakers and the tablecloth under her arm. Hymie put the bottle away and returned to the front room and Morris rejoined him.

The Dodgers are winning. The end of the sixth.

You wanna sit on the porch?

No, no. This is fine. It's beginning to get a little cooler. Before you know it... He stopped himself. He was going to say winter will be here. *It's a lousy life,* said Morris. *You get up in the morning. You go to work. You come home, you eat supper and you go to bed. And for what? For the children? You think they appreciate it?*

Well, you gotta make a living.

For who? The politicians? That louse in the White House?

He's not a bad president.

They're all a bunch of crooks.

So what's the answer?

My rent went up fifteen dollars. Can you imagine that? Fifteen dollars. And I had to give Meyer a raise.

I thought he worked on commission.

He gets a commission, too. He's doing better than I am and I got all the headaches. And now it looks like I may have to have an operation. Ever since that accident my life has been miserable. Sometimes I wish they'd cut the damned thing off. And the way Tillie spoils those boys. Nothing is good enough. We never had those things when we grew up...bikes, cameras. It never stops. Irving's almost sixteen. You think he helps out in the store? Oh, no. He's got extracurricular activities. I can't get around like I used to. I'm telling you, Hymie, it's not worth the effort.

Hymie studied Morris' face...the troubled eyes, the wrinkled brow. Was he really that disgusted with life? The children's voices floated in from the kitchen full of laughter and joy. Then Frieda's voice firm and admonishing.

It's all crap, Hymie.

You wanna change places?

What do you mean? Morris looked at Hymie, puzzled.

When my four months are up you can take my place.

Morris looked non-plussed for a moment, then blushed.

I was only joking, said Hymie.

It'll work out all right. You wait and see. You leave it to Tillie, Morris continued uneasily.

Hymie smiled, gazed at Morris then rose and patted him on the shoulder. *You're a good man, Morris*, he said and he walked to the window and stood peering out. Tillie was coming down the street with Adam, arm in arm. They looked as if they'd been friends for years. Frieda came into the living room without her apron. She had put on some lipstick and combed her air.

Sit down, sit down, said Morris. *You haven't stopped working.*

Would you like some fruit?

I couldn't eat another bite.

You hardly ate a thing.

I don't eat that much in a week.

They sat in silence for a moment, then Morris broke the silence. *You've got two beautiful children*, he said. *And I'm sure you'll have lots of "nachas" from them.*

We'd better be going, Tillie announced as she came into the room with Adam.

You're going already? You just got here, said Frieda.

I got a card game. I forgot all about it when I said we would come. Before I go I want you to try on the pants. This to Hymie.

Hymie rose obediently and started for the back of the apartment, followed by Tillie. In the bedroom he hesitated.

What's the matter? asked Tillie. *Oh, for God sakes, I've seen you without any clothes on at all. Put on the pants and don't be such a fool.* Hymie scowled, took off his trousers and put on the new ones. *They look fine,* said Tillie. *Turn around,* she ordered. He turned around.

So what did Adam say? he asked.

About what?

About what!!

He's gonna do what he can for you. There's nothing to worry about.

Hymie sighed in disgust.

Listen, Hymie, he's an angel. He's not just anybody. Right now he can't do a thing. But things can change from day to day. You've got over three months, so stop worrying. I want you to bring him to the store next week and I'm gonna give him a suit, and I'm not gonna charge him. But don't say a thing to Morris, about not charging. You hear me?

I hear you.

Go show the pants to Frija.

Hymie heaved a sigh and marched into the front room for Frieda's inspection.

They look very nice, said Frieda.

That's a beautiful pair of pants, said Morris. *What do you say, Adam?*

Very nice, said Adam.

Hymie's going to bring you out to the store next week, said Tillie. *I want you to pick out a suit.*

Thank you, said Adam.

Wear them in good health, said Morris getting up from the sofa with some difficultly.

Did you pay Tillie for the pants? Frieda asked Hymie.

I don't do business on Sunday, Tillie said lightly. *You'll pay me next week.* And she tried to signal to Hymie with her eyes that she didn't want Morris present when Hymie paid for the trousers. *We gotta go. Frija, you're gonna come over to my house one of these days and give me a cooking lesson.*

You don't need no cooking lesson.

And I want you to make a potato kugel, just for me.

Tell me when.

And a sponge cake. You promised me. I've having the game at my place next week.

I'll send it over with Hymie.

That's a promise.

I told you I'd make you a cake and I will.

Tillie kissed Frieda then Hymie. *Where are the children?*

They're outside, said Frieda. *I'll call them in.*

Let them alone. I'll see them outside. Adam, it's been a pleasure, said Tillie. She hesitated for a moment then kissed Adam firmly on the cheek. After all he did it first.

Same here, said Adam, looking slightly flustered.

Frieda and Hymie saw Tillie and Morris to the door and as Frieda closed the door after them she looked at Hymie and asked very softly, *What did Tillie say?*

Nothing.

Nothing?

Nothing.

I knew it. But when Tillie makes up her mind... She didn't say anything?

Adam said he couldn't do anything for me right now. But maybe things'll change.

All right. So what did we lose? said Frieda and she went into the front room. *Can I get you anything, Adam? Some fruit maybe.*

I couldn't eat a thing. Thank you.

If you'll excuse me for a minute. I've still got things to do.

Yes, of course.

And Frieda went back into the kitchen.

I'm sorry you had to waste a dinner on me, Adam said to Hymie.

Don't be foolish, said Hymie. *My wife wanted you over for dinner. That's all.*

If I could help you, Hymie, you know that I would.

I know, I know.

Where are the children?

They're outside.

Do you mind if I go outside for a while?

Go right ahead.

Adam went out the front door and Hymie joined Frieda in the kitchen. He sat down at the table and, to his surprise, Frieda sat down at the table across from him. *I was thinking,* she said. *Your mother's an old woman. She hasn't been well. How much time has she got?*

You wanna ask my mother?

Maybe not ask her. Maybe if we just let her know what's what.

That would be like asking her.

Not necessarily. I mean... Were you planning to keep it a secret? After all, I think she ought to know.

Besides, by time you write her and by the time she answers... Three weeks. Maybe four. I'll send it airmail.

I don't know.

She'd be doing a "mitzvah".

I don't know.

If you don't want me to, I won't.

If you just tell her maybe...

That's all I would do.

After a moment. *Do what you think best.*

Why don't we go for a ride somewhere? I've been cooped up in the house all week.

Where do you wanna go?

I don't know. It's a beautiful day. Let's go for a ride in the park.

All right, so we'll go for a ride.

We'll find a way, Hymie. We'll find a way. She patted his hands which were clasped on the table, and went to lock the back door.

CHAPTER SIX

UNCLE SAM AND AUNT ROSE

Hymie rose from the table and went outside to gather up Adam and the children. Frieda closed all the windows and locked the front door. On the porch she met Hymie coming back into the house.

I've got my new pants on.

So wear them.

My keys are in the other pants.

Hymie went back into the house for his keys and wallet and joined Frieda, Adam and the children at the car. Rachel was jumping up and down with excitement. *We're going for a ride,* she chanted. *We're going for a ride.*

Did you lock the door? asked Frieda.

Yes, I locked the door, Hymie replied, opened the doors of the car and got in. Adam sat in back with the children and Frieda sat up front with Hymie.

Where do you wanna go? he asked.

Let's go to the park.

Yes, yes, the park, echoed Rachel. *The park, the park!*

Tsk! The children should change their clothes, said Frieda.

Oh, Mother, Nathan protested. *We'll be careful.*

I won't dirty my dress. I promise, said Rachel.

All right. Let's go.

And down Nye Avenue they rode, the children peering excitedly out of the window. Adam sat looking dreamily into space, into another world, perhaps. Hymie's eyes were on the road but his mind was journeying back, back to Poland, the family farm, the dirt roads, the outdoor smells...and his mother. She had aged considerably the last time he'd seen her. Of course, his father had just died and she was in mourning. Nevertheless her face had been worn and care-lined and, yes, old, under that rather young looking wig that the Jewish women traditionally wore over their shorn locks. She'd been so happy to see him and made such a fuss over him. But it had been difficult for her to get around, even then. Was she bedridden now? He didn't even know. What would she think when she received Frieda's letter? The family looked for good news from America. How could he saddle them with this disaster? Maybe he ought to write the letter himself. What difference did it make?

Frieda spoke for both of them and, long ago, had assumed the task of the family correspondence. Besides women were so much better at that sort of thing...domestic things like births and death.

The playground, the playground! cried Rachel. *Let's go to the playground!*

Sit down and behave yourself, admonished Frieda.

Can't we go to the playground? Rachel persisted.

Yes, we'll go to the playground. Let's take them to the playground. Hymie? Hymie!

What?

The children want to go to the playground.

So we'll go to the playground.

Frieda studied her husband and sighed. He was healthy and alive and it couldn't happen. They had been through so many crises together...money problems, illnesses. They had weathered them all. It was cooler than she had thought. She should have brought a sweater. She rolled the window up just a little. The smell of fresh grass and trees. She drank them in. Farm life back in Poland had been hard, but it had had its little rewards. She missed the green growing things.

They were riding through the park now. Weequahic Park, large and sprawling, but well kept. They had entered the park near the lake which was dotted with row boats. Cars everywhere. People sitting on the grass. Picnicking on the grass. Children running about. Some men were playing baseball. They drove slowly by the lake.

Could we take a ride on a boat? asked Nathan.

No boat! said Frieda adamantly. (Even a ride in a rowboat was suggestive of traveling and Frieda had this phobia. Let's talk about something pleasant, she would say.)

Why not? asked Nathan.

I said no boat!

Let's go on a boat! chimed Rachel.

I thought you wanted to go the playground, Frieda parried.

If they wanna go on a boat..., Hymie started to say.

I said, no boat! and Frieda looked at him furiously. And that was the end of that. Besides the rippling water with the dancing sunlight was slowly passing into the distance. Gone. The lake was gone. Another adventure unfulfilled. The children groaned with disappointment. Suddenly the lake appeared again. An inlet, dark and mysterious.

Look at the ducks, said Nathan.

And they all (except Hymie, whose eyes were on the road) watched the ducks swim about.

We had ducks like that on our farm, said Frieda.

They look good enough to eat, said Nathan diabolically, looking evilly at Rachel.

Mommy, he's teasing me.

So don't pay attention.

Mmmm. Roast duck.

Mommy!

Nathan, stop it, said Frieda.

Mommy, he's tickling me, cried Rachel.

If you two don't behave yourself we're going back home, Frieda said.

There was silence. They were now driving behind the large stadium.

Where's the playground? asked Rachel.

We're going there, we're going there, said Frieda.

They came to the soft rolling hills and the road was thickly shaded by the trees which were still green and full. Suddenly they passed an open space and there, at the top of a hill, was a classic looking building, small yet dignified and, somehow, ominous. It looked like a mausoleum and Hymie shuddered slightly.

Are you cold? asked Frieda.

No.

There's the playground, said Nathan.

There's the playground, echoed. Rachel.

There's no place to park. We'll have to go further down. said Hymie.

The playground, the playground! Rachel protested as they drove on.

Oh, shut up! said Nathan.

Don't talk to your sister like that, said Hymie. There! He had made his contribution to family discipline. A parking place was found a short distance from the playground and they piled out of the car into the cool, fresh smelling air. *Oh, this air smells so good*, said Frieda. *What a pleasure!* A thrill of gratification surged through Hymie. For one sweet moment his wife was happy and was actually willing to admit it. A rare, historical occasion! *Let's go on the swings*, said Rachel and she took Adam's hand. *Watch the cars!* warned Frieda. They all crossed the road and walked toward the playground. Rachel let go of Adam's hand, ran ahead, slipped and fell, scraping her knee. *Rachel!* shouted Frieda. Rachel stood silently, waiting for the rest of them to catch up with her. *Let me see your knee*, said Frieda. *It's all right. It's not bleeding*, said Rachel. *Walk. Don't run*, said Frieda. Rachel took Adam's hand and walked sedately beside him. The playground came into sight and there were the swings. Suddenly Adam took Nathan's hand with his free hand, shouted, *Come on. Let's go!* and the three of them ran to the swings. Frieda looked at Hymie and shrugged. How was one to chide an angel? Especially an angel from whom they were expecting big favors, hoping for, at any rate. One big one, that is.

Rachel ignored the small swings, with the protective bars and climbed onto one of the adult swings. Nathan climbed onto another one. Adam pushed Rachel and she pumped furiously with her chubby little legs, her eyes glowing with the effort. The angel pushed Nathan once but the boy protested that he could manage himself, and so he did, swinging high into the air.

Not so high, shouted Frieda.

I'm all right, called Nathan.

Mommy, mommy! Look at me! cried Rachel.

I see, I see.

Daddy, daddy! Look at me!

Very good, said Hymie and he turned to his wife. *You wanna walk around?*

Where should we walk?

Hymie shrugged.

All right. Let's walk.

Adam readily agreed to look after the children. Indeed he looked like a child himself. And Hymie and Frieda strolled off. *There's a garden over there*, observed Frieda, and they walked toward the large flower garden, Frieda hungrily sniffing the air. Hymie felt the urge to take his wife's hand. Frieda sensed this and felt the urge to respond, but neither of them reached out. After thirteen years of marriage they were still awkward with one another. They wandered through the garden looking at the colorful flowers...the roses, the tulips, the gladiolas. A riot of color. A vast bouquet of sweet smelling aromas. A bee buzzed by and Frieda stiffened. *You wanna sit down?* asked Hymie. *So let's sit down.* And they sat on a bench and looked about. People strolled by in pairs. A little boy passed, bouncing a ball. The boy's mother shouted after him to come back. Such a lazy, peaceful afternoon. The sun was gold in the sky. The clouds were orange and crimson against the blue.

We should be going home soon, said Frieda after a while.

We just got here.

The bee continued to buzz nearby. It was making Frieda nervous. *It'll go away. Just sit still.* Hymie wanted to talk about the future. Suppose he couldn't find a substitute? What then? He looked at Frieda, but she turned away. Obviously she didn't want to talk about it. She didn't want to talk about it and she didn't want to think about it. It was getting a little chilly. Hymie looked at his watch. Six o'clock. They sat on the bench in the middle of the garden, not quite at ease, and yet they didn't want to leave. It was peaceful here, so peaceful. Who knew what the future held? Finally Frieda said, *We'd better go.*

All right. Let's go. They rose reluctantly and slowly found their way back to the playground. Nathan was still on his swing, swinging away. Rachel had found the slide. *Mommy! Daddy! Look at me!* She was at the top of the slide. Frieda caught her breath. Rachel sat down and slid to the bottom of the slide where Adam caught her and lifted her into the air, shouting triumphantly. Rachel laughed with delight. *Again, again!* she cried. Nathan joined Hymie and Frieda. *Why don't you go up there?* Hymie asked.

I'm too big for that.

Let's go on the seesaw, Rachel called.

We're going home, said Frieda.

Rachel groaned with disappointment.

We just got here, said Nathan.

Aren't you hungry? asked Frieda.

Not me, said Nathan.

Not me, echoed Rachel.

You want to stay a while? Frieda asked Hymie.

It's up to you.

You want to go to the movies, don't you? And I thought we might stop up and see Uncle Sam and Aunt Rose.

Are they expecting us?

I told them we might drop by. They invited us over this afternoon. I should have asked them to dinner, but it would have been too much.

So let's go.

We won't stay long.

Are we going? asked Rachel.

Yes, we're going, said Nathan, *And we're going to stop and see Uncle Sam and Aunt Rose.*

Only you've got to behave, said Frieda. *No noise and no running around. Uncle Sam isn't feeling too well.*

What's the matter with him? asked Nathan.

He's sick.

Well, if he's not feeling well, he's sick. But what kind of sickness has he got?

I didn't ask.

They walked back to the car in silence. Even the children seemed unusually quiet. *It's getting chilly,* said Frieda as they drove out of the park, leaving the sun behind them it seemed. Uncle Sam and Aunt Rose lived in a large apartment house just around the corner from the Benders, where Clinton Place curved onto Wolcott Terrace.   It was a new apartment building. Red brick with a large white doorway and white window frames. The children passed it often and looked at it with awe, since it was the only apartment building in the area. Hymie parked the car in front of their own house and they all walked around the corner. He had suggested that they leave the children at home but Frieda rejected the idea.

But if he's sick...

She'll want to see the children.

The five of them entered the foyer of white marble. (Was it really marble? Nathan wondered.) Hymie rang the bell. There was no answer.

Are you sure they're home? Hymie asked.

They're home, they're home. Ring again.

Hymie rang again and the door buzzer responded. Nathan dashed to the door and pushed it open. *I got it, I got it,* he called.

Shhhhh, said Rachel, giving Nathan a piece of his own medicine.

Shhhhh, yourself.

They walked through the elegant lobby to the elevator and Nathan went to push the button. *Let me push it,* said Rachel. Nathan looked at his sister and deliberately pushed the button, and the elevator door opened.

Why didn't you let me?

You're too young.

All right, children. Remember what I said, said Frieda.

They all entered the elevator.

You wanna push the button? asked Nathan.

Yes.

You can't reach it.

I can reach it, I can reach it.
Hymie picked the child up.
What floor? the girl asked.
Five, said Frieda. And Rachel pushed the button. The door slid closed. The motor started and the elevator began to rise.
This sure is a slow elevator, Nathan commented.
There's no rush, said Hymie.
There is if you want to get to the movies tonight. The last show starts at eight thirty.
There's plenty of time, said Frieda. *We're just going to stop in for a minute.*
Fifth floor. All out, announced Nathan. And they all filed out of the elevator into the newly painted, rather barren looking hallway.
Apartment K, said Frieda.
It's this way, said Nathan, inspecting the doors and leading them down the hallway. They stopped in front of the door marked K. *Shall I ring the bell?* he asked of no one in particular and proceeded to ring the doorbell. There was a long pause.
Ring it again, said Frieda. *Maybe they didn't hear.*
The door finally opened and Aunt Rose stood in the doorway in a colorful housecoat, looking quite glamorous despite the puffy eyes. *I'm sorry. I was taking a nap,* she apologized in that husky cigarette voice. *Maybe we should have called,* said Frieda.
No, no. I was hoping you would come. Come in. Please
And they entered the apartment. It was elegantly furnished and dimly lit. Aunt Rose led the way, turning on several lamps. *Come in here,* she said, ushering them into the living room. There was a Persian rug on the floor. The venetian blinds were drawn. *Sam is getting dressed. He hasn't been feeling well, and he needs all the rest he can get.* Frieda introduced Adam to Aunt Rose and they shook hands.
You're looking very well, Hymie, said Aunt Rose. *I heard you were sick.*
I'm feeling fine.
There's a lot going around. It's the change in the weather. She looked longingly at the children. *You look so pretty today, Rachel.*
We were at the park.
Were you, dear?
I rode on the swing and I slid down the slide.
Do you like going to the park?
Oh, yes.

*Maybe you'd like to come to the park with your Aunt Rose and
Uncle Sam sometime. Would you like that?*

All right.

*And how about you, Nathan? Would you like to come to the park
with us?*

All right.

You're getting to be a big boy now. What grade are you in?

The seventh.

You'll be graduating soon.

Next year.

*I have some cookies. Would you children like some cookies and
milk?*

You don't have to, said Frieda.

I got them especially. Would you like some, Rachel?

Rachel looked at Frieda.

What are you looking at me for? Would you like some cookies?

Yes, said Rachel shyly.

How about you, Nathan?

Okay.

*Come into the kitchen. Who else would like some milk, or coffee
maybe. How about you, Adam?*

I wouldn't mind some coffee.

Good. Come along.

Are you coming? Adam asked Hymie.

No, no. You go ahead.

And all, except Hymie, went into the kitchen. In the living room
he sat down carefully on a fancy looking chair and looked about. He
wondered how much money Uncle Sam really had. He knew they lived
lavishly. Aunt rose liked nice things and insisted on having them. They
took vacations and went out to restaurants. Hymie couldn't remember the
last time he'd eaten in a restaurant.

Uncle Sam came in from the bedroom wearing trousers and a
silk dressing gown. He was tall, dark and sad looking with a long
creased face and brooding eyes. His hair was streaked with gray. *Hello,
Hymie. How are you?* he asked in his deep, gravelly voice and he offered
his hand. Hymie shook the cold, limpid hand and wondered, as he often
did in Uncle Sam's presence, what heavy burden the man carried inside
of him. Uncle Sam never laughed. Frieda did neither, but there was
something funereal about his uncle.

Can I get you a drink?

No, thank you, Hymie heard himself say to his own astonishment.

How about a cigar?

I'll have a cigarette, if you don't mind, said Hymie and he pulled his pack from his pocket. They both lit up and sat smoking. *Rose was telling me some strange things.*

You mean about my sickness?

Yes.

Hymie repeated the whole story and Uncle Sam listened with great interest. There were times when he looked vaguely into the distance and Hymie thought that his uncle's mind was wandering, but then Uncle Sam would ask a question that showed clearly he was following his nephew's story very closely.

Suppose you found a substitute? What would you do then?

I don't know. I suppose I'd tell Adam. He'd know what to do.

Aunt Rose came into the room. *Would you like some coffee, Hymie?*

No, thank you.

Sam?

Uncle Sam shook his head.

How are you feeling?

Uncle Sam shrugged noncommittally and Aunt Rose went back into the kitchen.

How am I feeling? What's the use of telling her? If I feel a little better for a while, it doesn't last very long.

What does the doctor say?

He doesn't say anything. He uses me as a guinea pig. Let's try this. Let's try that.

Why don't you try another doctor?

I've tried them all. It's no pleasure getting up in the morning, I tell you. If it weren't for Rose... And Uncle Sam looked dreamily into the distance.

I'm sorry to hear that.

You're a good boy, Hymie. You're like the son I never had. I don't want to say anything now, you understand. Hymie nodded, not daring to say a word. *Drop by my place next week. Make in the middle of the week.*

Hymie nodded again, not daring to hope. Frieda came into the room. *If we're going to the movies,* she said, *we'd better get started.* Hymie rose and looked apologetically at his uncle.

That's all right, said Uncle Sam. *Enjoy yourself while you can.*
How are you feeling? asked Frieda?
You're looking well, Frieda.
Thank you.
Enjoy the movie.
Thank you, said Hymie.

The children came into the room, followed by Adam and Aunt Rose. *Say hello to Uncle Sam,* Frieda said to the children, and the children came to Uncle Sam and shook his hand. *Hello, Uncle Sam,* said Rachel. *Hello, Uncle Sam,* said Nathan. Uncle Sam smiled at them, but one could see that it was an effort.

This is Adam, said Frieda.

How do you do, said Uncle Sam with a little more interest.

We'd better go, said Frieda and they all moved to the door, leaving Uncle Sam standing in the middle of the living room. *Thank you for coming,* said Aunt Rose.

I hope he feels better. said Frieda.

Good-by, Hymie. Good-bye, children, said Aunt Rose and she kissed them both. She stood in the doorway watching Hymie and his brood move down the hallway to the elevator, then she shut the door of her apartment.

Rose hesitated before returning to the living room and facing her husband. Sam had never been a jolly man, but he had always been charming and outgoing with a rather wry sense of humor. But this terrible nagging illness had changed all that. There were times when she blamed all the different medications, but without them there would be pain. There was no hope, she knew that. The initial operation had been a success but then several years later the dreaded disease had returned. If only they could enjoy the little time that they had left.

Rose loved Sam's family and since she had no close relatives, except for one sister who lived in Rochester, she felt quite close to them. But she also had the perspective of a native born American. This desperate, driven need to make a success in a strange environment was also part of Sam's make-up but she saw to it that it was kept under control. She insisted that his evenings be free. She insisted on a social and a cultural life. She read a great deal and even got Sam to read a book now and then. They attended the theatre (in New York on Broadway, no less), an occasional concert or a museum. But now that he was in the grip of this terrible disease all that had come to a halt. The effect of the disease on his body, awful as it was, was even more

destructive on his mental outlook. All the joy had gone out of his life.
There were times Rose felt that she was living with a corpse, and she
would shudder. The encounter with the children had been an embracing
tonic. She was sorry she hadn't insisted on adoption but for years they
had kept hoping and trying, and then, when the illness made it's initial
appearance the subject was dropped. *Did you get a good rest?* Rose
asked as she reentered the living room.

Sam nodded.

Would you like to go for a walk? It's still nice out.

Maybe later.

The card game is later.

No card game. Not tonight.

It's just across the hall.

I'm not up to it.

It'll take your mind off...

Not tonight. You go. You don't have to stay here. Go.

All right. I'd better change.

Why? That's a very nice gown.

It's a housecoat.

It's very pretty.

*I'll change later. I said I'd help her with the food. She makes
such a fuss with the food.*

Go ahead.

She kissed him on the forehead, started for the door and stopped.
Sam, dear, I'd like to take the children out some Sunday.

Fine.

We'll take them for a ride and then to the park.

Fine.

You're sure you don't want to play?

I'm sure.

I'll be back to change.

All right.

Rose left the apartment and went to join her neighbor across the
hall. Sam sat looking out the window, gazing at the darkening sky,
trying not to think about the future, trying not to worry about what was
to happen sooner or later. He'd made all the preparations for the
inevitable that was humanly possible and his thoughts turned to his
nephew.

*****

In the street Adam walked ahead with the children. Hymie and Frieda trailed behind. *It's a shame they never had any children,* said Frieda. *He doesn't look good,* she added.

He was never really well ever since I came here.

Did you know him in Brostek?

I was very young when he left.

He's been good to you.

It was beginning to get dark. The street light on the corner of Clinton Place and Nye Avenue came on. *The days are getting shorter,* said Frieda as they entered the house through the front door. *You better get going if you wanna make that movie,* said Nathan. Frieda wondered whether she ought to invite Adam to come with them and took Hymie aside. *So ask him,* said Hymie, which Frieda did.

You're not taking the children, are you? asked Adam.

No, no.

Then I'll stay here with them.

You won't forget to bring the hot dogs, said Nathan.

We'll see, said Frieda. *It all depends on what time we get out.*

I want hot works, said Nathan.

I want sweet works, said Rachel.

All right, all right, said Frieda. *Are you ready?*

I'm ready, said Hymie.

Maybe I'd better take a sweater.

So take a sweater.

Frieda went into the bedroom and returned with a sweater which she draped over her shoulders. *Now behave yourself,* said Frieda, *And don't give Adam any trouble.*

We won't, said Rachel.

And Hymie and Frieda went off to the movies.

CHAPTER SEVEN

THE MOVIES

Shall I take the car? Hymie asked as they came onto the porch.

For three blocks?

I'm on my feet all day.

So take the car.

All right, let's walk.

Let's take the car. I don't want you complaining afterwards.

They got into the car. Hymie made a U turn and drove along Wolcott Terrace toward Hawthorne Avenue.

What did Uncle Sam have to say? asked Frieda.

The same old thing. It was less than half an hour since he'd spoken to his uncle and he wasn't quite sure what had transpired. Or was it that he didn't want to raise his hopes too high?

What are you thinking? asked Frieda.

Nothing. I'll park here.

That's what he thinks of me, nothing, thought Frieda.

Hymie drew up to the right side of Wolcott Terrace and parked a few yards from Hawthorne Avenue. As Frieda got out of the car she took a deep breath and sighed. What a beautiful night and what a shame to spend it inside a stuffy theatre. She would much rather take a walk. She felt so alone. Hymie had all his companions at "the place" and she had no one, no one she could really pour her heart out to. There was Tillie, of course, but Tillie was not always that sympathetic and, besides, Tillie had problems of her own. Hymie was her husband. They lived together. They slept together. And yet they were strangers. What did she know about him? And what did he know about her? Did he think about her? Did he think about her?! That's a question? She was a servant! That's what she was.

What's the matter? asked Hymie.

Nothing, she said. If he thought so little of her, the hell with him.

Hymie sighed. She was angry about something. *I thought you wanted to go to the movies.*

What difference does it make what I want?

He would never understand her. Never in a million years. He did everything in his power to please her. He supported her and the children without a murmur. He tried not to burden her with unnecessary responsibilities, knowing how nervous she could get. All right, maybe he wasn't perfect, but when he was gone, she'd be sorry, very sorry. She'd appreciate him then.

She had strained herself to the utmost preparing that dinner. Day and night worrying every minute that everything would come out just right. The dinner had been a huge success. Had he given her one word of thanks? He couldn't say, "Frija, you've done a good job." The arrogance of the man!

Do you want to go to the movies or not?

We're here. Let's go.

He stepped up to the box office, bought two tickets and they entered the lobby of the theatre. They didn't even know what was playing, Frieda thought. Just go. It didn't matter. He would go to see the story of the crucifixion so long as it was up on the screen.

Would you like something to drink? Hymie asked.

They had entered the theatre and were standing in the back.

We have soda home.

You want some candy?

You want some, get some. He has money to spend on candy and when I ask him for an extra penny for the house...

Hymie sighed. He sighted some seats in a row about two thirds from the screen. *Is this all right?* he whispered.

Fine.

They took their seats and sat watching the screen.

This is it, thought Hymie. My night on the town. Sitting in a local movie house with a surly wife. Is this the glory that the golden myth of America had promised? Wealth? Power? Success? Here he sat, in a darkened theatre in an alien country, alone and forsaken. Alone, alone. Forever alone. The friends he had at the store. Were they really his friends? And his family. They accepted him because he was part of the family. And his children and his wife. Would they really mourn him when he was gone? Oh, yes. Maybe when they got hungry. Maybe when the rent came around.

The co-feature was ending and the news came on. President Roosevelt signed a Social Security Bill. If Hymie lived long enough he could collect retirement pay from the government. (Forget about it!) Mussolini was marching Italian troops into Abyssinia. King George was celebrating his silver jubilee in London. And, of course, there were the inevitable bathing beauties in Atlantic City. Frieda glanced over at Hymie to see his reaction. (What is she looking for? Hymie thought.)

A Bugs Bunny cartoon came on. This Frieda could do without. Finally the main feature came on. "Of Human Bondage" with Leslie Howard (whom Frieda liked, refined and sensitive) and Bette Davis. The husband and wife became absorbed in the story of a man's obsession with a woman unworthy of him. Frieda both marveled and was taken aback by what romantic passion could do to a human being. Hymie understood, only too well, how destructive a woman could be. Frieda noted, with surprise, that her husband nodded only once during the entire film. Why he was so anxious to go to the movies and then, when they got there, he would fall asleep...this was a puzzlement to her. Frieda turned away when Bette Davis, was taken from her room on a stretcher, dead from starvation. A woman alone in the world did not have a chance. Hymie was glad to see that Leslie Howard ended up with a nice, sweet girl. But then that girl would become a wife.

The second feature began and Hymie grew restless. He enjoyed Westerns, as a rule, but his mind was too full. *I'm going to smoke*, he whispered to Frieda and went to the back of the theatre. He started to light up, remembered that no smoking was allowed there and went into the men's room. He stood smoking next to the open window in order to avoid inhaling the strong smell of camphor. If Uncle Sam didn't come through, maybe his mother would. There was still plenty of time. Maybe Adam would regain his influence. He put out the cigarette and went back to his seat.

Did you enjoy your cigarette? asked Frieda sarcastically, and then regretted it when she observed that her husband seemed to be in a good mood. He'd received some good news. When? From whom? The man was absolutely infuriating. The Western rolled on. The horses rode furiously. The cowboys shot at one another. Some cattle had been rustled, Frieda gathered, but all the cowboys looked alike. *Do you want to stay?* she asked.

You want to go?

You're not even watching the picture.

You want to go, let's go.

So they rose and started to leave.

Frieda had to go back for her sweater, naturally.

Outside on the street Frieda inhaled the cool night air.

You wanna get the hot dogs? Hymie asked.

The children are expecting it, said Frieda.

So they got into the car and drove up Hawthorne Avenue four blocks to Cohen's, a store that specialized in kosher hot dogs and knishes. Frieda was sure that whatever Hymie was keeping from her had

to do with Uncle Sam. As they pulled up in front of Cohen's Frieda
broke the silence. *Are you going to tell me, or aren't you?*

Tell you what?

What Uncle Same said to you.

*There's nothing to tell. He wants me to drop in to see him next
week.*

Why?

He didn't say.

You have no idea why?

He said that I was like the son he never had.

He knows the whole story?

You're asking me? Didn't you talk to Aunt Rose?

You think, maybe...?

I told you what he said.

All right, all right. But he must have something to tell you.

He'll tell me what he has to tell me when he tells me.

I'm just asking.

So, I told you. You want me to come inside with you?

Stay here. You want one?

All right. Mustard and sauerkraut.

But Frieda didn't move. She sat waiting and Hymie realized that
he hadn't given her any money. He reached in his pocket and pulled out
a dollar bill.

Hot dogs have gone up. And I'll have to get one for Adam.

He handed her another dollar.

You want a liver knish?

Make it a liver knish.

Frieda got out of the car and went into the store.

Hymie sat at the wheel, peering into the dark of the cool, fading
summer. His head was spinning. He hadn't wanted to talk about it.
Uncle Sam's words had been a spark of hope, a spark he wanted to nurse
inside himself. What a devil she was! Hymie felt, as he had so many
times since the beginning of his marriage, that his individuality had been
threatened. Was he or was he not Hymie Bender? Or was he just a
husband and a father with no identity of his own? He thought of his dead
father and wondered if he, too had faced this very same problem.

Frieda opened the door of the car, got in and slammed the door
after her. She held a large paper bag on her lap. *They didn't have liver
so I got a couple of potato knishes.*

All right.

You're angry?

I'm not angry.

Frieda raised her eyebrows and said nothing.

You have to know everything. Why must you know everything? Suppose I wanted to keep something to myself? Do I ask you every move you make, everything you say, everything you think?

Never!

So why do you have to pick my brains all the time?

There's nothing much to pick.

Hymie glanced over at Frieda. She was a damned attractive woman. Infuriating, but attractive. He drove through the darkened tree-lined streets, across Leslie Street and then left down Nye Avenue. In all probability he would be dead before the end of the year and all he could think about was making love to Frieda. The woman had just invaded his inmost thoughts, the last outpost of his privacy, and here he wanted to make love to her.

Where are you going?

He had just passed the house. Hymie applied the brakes, backed up and parked in front of the house. This was not a mansion, he thought, but maybe he was not cut out to be a millionaire. The friendship...friendship?...the good will of his fellow man meant more to him than the extra dollar. He would not water his drinks, like one of his colleagues did. A friend of his, who had a butcher shop, would press his finger on the scale when he weighed the meat. Such tactics were not for him.

You're "fetrocht" tonight.

They were sitting in the parked car in front of the house. Hymie was staring ahead through the windshield.

You wanna talk? asked Frieda.

What is there to talk about?

Frieda sighed, got out of the car and started up the alley to the back door. Hymie sighed and followed her.

The light was on in the kitchen. Adam had the radio on the sewing machine turned on very low and was listening to it. The door to the children's bedroom was very slightly ajar.

It was thrown open before Frieda had even set the bag on the table. The children burst into the kitchen, almost bumping into Hymie entering from the outside. The hot dogs and the knishes, wrapped in wax paper, were set out on the table and the five of them took seats around the kitchen table. (Nathan brought in the extra chair from the dining room.) The children, in their pajamas, eagerly unwrapped their hot dogs and bit into them and the adults followed suit. Nathan said, *Mmmm.*

Yummy, as he bit into the juicy morsel smeared with mustard and smothered in hot relish and sauerkraut. Rachel murmured, *Mmmmmmm,* a little sleepily and munched happily on her treat. The others followed suit. Soda was brought in from the ice box in the pantry, glasses were produced and the delicacies were washed down.

That was good, said Nathan and he began to pump Frieda about the movie. Was it good? Who was in it? Was Bette Davis good? Was Leslie Howard good? Who else was in it? How was the other picture? Frieda answered the questions the best she could. The children were hustled back to bed, the trash gathered up and thrown into the garbage pail and the glasses placed in the sink.

I'll take you back, said Hymie to Adam. *The room is paid for already so you might as well use it.*

He can sleep on the couch already, said Frieda.

Since I have to open up in the morning, maybe I'd better go back, said Adam.

I'll take you down.

I'll be ready in a minute, said Adam, and he went into the bathroom.

Frieda rinsed out the glasses and, to her surprise, Hymie offered to dry.

So, shall I write to your mother or not?

So write her.

I'll just tell her the situation, that's all.

Whatever you think. (Hymie didn't want to dwell on the subject. It made him very uneasy.)

All set, said Adam as he emerged from the bathroom.

Hymie kissed Frieda and left with Adam.

It was late but Frieda wasn't sleepy. She got out the writing paper, the pen and ink, sat down at the kitchen table and started to write a letter to Hymie's mother.

CHAPTER EIGHT

ADAM'S SUIT

The beginning of the week passed uneventfully. With two full time helpers in the bar Hymie did not have to work so hard, but this only served to make him uneasy. He looked healthier and more rested, but he was becoming more and more preoccupied, more absent-minded. There were times when he forgot about the Sword of Damocles that hung over his head but, subconsciously, it influenced every move he made, every thought, every emotion. He played little games with himself. As he drove off to work one afternoon he glanced at little Rachel sitting on the porch with a book, and said to himself, "If she doesn't kiss me good-bye, no one will come to my rescue." The child looked up, smiled and waved. Was that a good sign or a bad? As he drove past the corner of Goodwin Avenue he saw Nathan strolling home from Hebrew school. And there is my son, he said to himself. I'll never see him again, unless he looks up and waves to me. But Nathan was looking up at the sky, for some strange reason, and never noticed his father. Gone. Gone. Forever gone. And then there were the traffic lights. If I pass that green light before it turns yellow, I will be saved. He passed the light before it changed, but it was a hollow triumph because he didn't really believe in the game. He kept feeling that he ought to do something. But he was doing something, wasn't he? He was waiting. And that's what life was all about, wasn't it? Waiting, waiting, waiting. Waiting for Frieda to join him in America from Poland. Wait for his liquor license. Waiting for checks to clear. Waiting for Nathan to be born. And now he was waiting for Uncle Sam to make up his mind. He was waiting to hear from his mother. He swerved to avoid an oncoming car which he hadn't noticed coming around the corner. If he weren't careful, he wouldn't have to wait much longer.

Adam was a little more cheerful since the Sunday dinner and he was fast becoming a great favorite with all the customers, much to Phil's chagrin. (Phil was not very popular.) The men were sometimes baffled by the angel's lack of interest in the subject of sex, but Adam's charm and good humor always left them warm and friendly. They nicknamed him "the professor". As for Hymie, he and Adam had become like brothers. Hymie was more relaxed in the angel's company than he had ever been with anyone, including Frieda and any member of his family.

There was no sense of rivalry between them, no emotional claims, just friendship and good will. Adam helped to make this difficult time for him bearable, and Hymie knew that if the angel could help him he most certainly would. But there were moments, it's true, when Hymie had his doubts. Doubts about everyone and everything. The fact of the matter was he was becoming rather cynical. His customers were beginning to notice it, too. His sarcasm was no longer as amiable and as light hearted as it used to be. Obviously something was troubling him. Phil didn't seem to know what it was, nor did Adam...or so he said.

Early in the afternoon, on the following Wednesday, Hymie and Adam piled into the Chevrolet and started for Orange to pick out a suit for Adam.

You're not very cheerful these days, remarked Adam, after they'd been driving for a while.

What have I got to be cheerful about?

No luck?

Hymie told Adam about Uncle Sam and the letter to his mother.

Adam was silent for a moment and then he said, *Maybe you could use some help.*

Like what?

Maybe if some of the men in "the place" knew about it...

I don't like everyone to know my business.

This is an emergency.

I'll wait to see what Uncle Sam has to say.

When do you see him?

This afternoon. When we get back.

Adam was frankly baffled by Hymie's attitude and, by what seemed to be, the attitude of men in general. Granted there were joys to be found here on earth, but death was inevitable. Of course, it would be nice to have death come at the end of a full life, but surely men learned quickly enough that one couldn't pick and choose. And yet they clung so desperately to the breath of life. Was it fear of the unknown? Were they so loath to leave one another. The flesh was burdensome, was it not? And life here on earth wasn't that fulfilling. Adam was beginning to see the design of his punishment.

It was almost mid-afternoon when they arrived at the Kaufman clothing emporium. The store was empty, except for Meyer, the salesman, and Tillie, who was in the back on the phone. Morris was at the doctor's. Meyer greeted Hymie warmly and led them back to Tillie.

Now look, Barry, two weeks okay. Three I can understand, you've got a lot of expenses. But you're two months behind. I've got to have something on account. No, my dear, I'm not gonna run after you. I'll expect a check in the mail by Saturday, the latest. Now don't give me that. Am I gonna get the money or not? Okay. That's better. Give my regards to your wife. And Tillie hung up.

What a dead beat! She looked rather coldly at Hymie. *How are you today?* Hymie shrugged. Tillie kissed her brother rather perfunctorily and shook hands with Adam. *It's good to see you again,* she said. *Meyer, take my friend out front and find him a nice suit. That grey pin stripe maybe.* And Meyer took Adam to the front of the store.

How are the children?

They're fine. What's wrong with Morris?

What's wrong with Morris!? It's his leg.

Are they gonna operate?

Who knows? They don't know themselves. Where we're going to get the money for an operation I don't know. Listen Hymie, I said you could have the suit for nothing, but Morris found out about it and he hit the ceiling. I've got to charge you something.

All right. So charge me.

It won't be more than cost price. You said your self business was picking up.

I said I'd pay for the suit.

You haven't found anybody? Have you looked around?

Hymie shrugged.

You've got to get off your ass and start looking.

What do you want me to do?

You could put an ad in the Jewish News.

You're joking, aren't you?

If I had time I would help you, but I've got a business to run, a cripple and two growing boys to take care of.

I wrote a letter to Mamma.

You what?!

Frieda did, that is.

And what did you tell her?

We told her what the situation was, that's all.

And you expect her...? I don't believe it.

It was Frieda's idea.

And you let her? You've got a hell of a nerve! Why didn't she write to her mother? I'm ashamed of you, Hymie. And asking poor Morris.

What are you talking about?

He told me all about it.

I was just joking.

Some joke! Oh, Hymie, Hymie, what am I gonna do with you?

How much do I owe you for the pants?

Give me five dollars.

Hymie took the money out of his pocket and gave it to her. *I don't want you to do me anymore favors.*

All right, all right. Calm down.

They went up front to look at Adam in the suit. Tillie looked him over critically, front and back and said finally, *Take it.*

What do you think? Adam asked Hymie.

You like it?

It's okay, Adam replied then turned to Tillie and Meyer. *Okay.*

Come in the back and I'll measure you for the cuffs, said Meyer.

Meyer and Adam went to the back of the store. Hymie and Tillie stood indecisively. Finally Tillie spoke. *I've got work to do.* She was about to go to the back of the store when the door opened and Morris limped in.

Well? asked Tillie. *What did they say?*

He wants to operate.

When?

In a couple of weeks.

He thinks it'll help?

He said if they don't operate I'll lose the leg. Morris limped up to Hymie and shook hands. *Hello, Hymie.*

I'm sorry to hear about your trouble, said Hymie.

I'd be better off without the damn thing. Did Adam find something?

The gray pin stripe, Tillie said.

That's a very good suit, Morris said. *Excuse me, Hymie. I've got to sit down. Come in the back.*

Morris limped to the desk in the back and sat in the swivel chair. Hymie and Tillie followed behind.

Where's Andy? Tillie asked.

He went home. He said he'd call you. (Andy was a good friend of the Kaufman's, a "goy" with a Jewish heart, who often did favors for them.)

How long will you be laid up? Did the doctor say? asked Tillie.

Six weeks, at least.

Tillie sighed.

Adam joined them at the desk. Morris extended his hand. *How are you, Adam?*

Fine. said the angel, shaking Morris' hand.

The bell rang in the front of the store. *That's a customer.* said Morris. *That's all right.*, said Tillie. *Meyer'll get it. I've got to go. I'm late already. Good-bye, Adam. I'm sure you'll enjoy the suit.* She shook Adam's hand. She made no move to kiss her brother, or even bid him good-bye She picked up her large black pocket book from the desk, gave some final instructions to Meyer and walked out the front door.

I've got to go too, said Hymie. *Good luck, Morris.* And he shook Morris' hand.

You, too, said Morris.

Adam shook hands with Morris and he and Hymie walked to the front of the store. Meyer left the customer, a heavy black woman, and joined them. *You think they know what they want?* said Meyer. *Good luck, Hymie. Adam.* Meyer shook hands with them both. *The suit should be ready by the end of the week. Tillie will let you know. Give my regards to Frieda.*

Thank you, said Hymie and, as he and Adam left the store, all he could think about was Uncle Sam.

CHAPTER NINE

UNCLE SAM'S DECISION

Hymie drove back to "the place" with Adam. He was just going to drop Adam off and go right to Uncle Sam's, but decided he'd better look in to make sure everything was all right. There were a few customers at the bar and they greeted him warmly. He would like to have stopped and chat, but he didn't want to delay the momentous meeting any longer. Frieda had left a message with Phil for him to call her as soon as he got in. He sighed, picked up the phone reluctantly and dialed. The place needs a coat of paint, he thought as he waited for his wife to answer the phone.

Hello?

Why did you call?

What did he say?

I didn't go yet.

When are you going?

I'm going now, as soon as I hang up.

Call me.

I'll call you, I'll call you.

Hymie...

What?

Drive carefully. And don't forget to call me.

Hymie hung up and smiled to himself. They'd pretended to put no faith in Uncle Sam's words, but the truth of the matter was they were really counting on hearing some good news.

I'll be back in an hour, he said to Phil then left the bar, got into the car and drove the few blocks to Raymond Boulevard where Uncle Sam had his place. He pulled into a side street and parked the car a few feet from the tavern.

Uncle Sam was behind the bar. There were two customers in the place. His uncle came over to greet him and shook hands. *How about a drink?* his uncle asked. Hymie shrugged his assent and Uncle Sam poured him a Scotch. *Sit down, Hymie.* They sat in a booth, Uncle Sam facing the bar so that he could keep an eye on it. Apparently he was there by himself.

How's Frieda, and the children?

They're fine.

That Nathan's getting to be a big boy. When's his bar mitzvah?

Soon. (How long was this going to go on?) *How are you feeling?* Hymie asked.

113

I feel a little better. The doctor gave me a new medicine and it seems to help. I'm thinking about selling the place, in case you know someone that wants to buy. Rose has been after me. I'll be sixty two next month. She wants me to retire.

How much are you asking?

Thirty thousand. That's the whole building, including the candy store.

If I hear of anybody, I'll let you know.

She wants to travel. I've got a little money put aside. If we live carefully we'll be all right. What's the weather like outside?

Very nice.

I'm taking the night off. We're going into New York to see a show. We ought to go to a show together someday. The four of us.

What show are you going to see?

I don't even know the name. It's a comedy.

A Jewish show?

No, no. It's on Broadway. She sent away for the tickets. You work too hard, Hymie. You ought to take a little time off. The time to enjoy yourself is now, when you're young. Excuse me.

A customer had come in and Uncle Sam got up to serve him. He returned to the booth a few minutes later. *It's going to start to be busy soon.*

You told me to drop by.

The truth of the matter is, Hymie, I wasn't feeling too good on Sunday and I thought... Well, you know... But things have changed.

I see.

I wish you the best. You know that, Hymie.

I better be getting back.

Let me know how things are going.

I will. Give my regards to Aunt Rose.

Rose would like to take the children out for a ride some time, if that's all right.

Any time.

The two men shook hands. Uncle Sam returned to the bar and watched Hymie leave. He tried not think about his nephew's plight. He tried to ignore the guilty pang that attacked his heart. His time was limited too and he owed that time to Rose. She'd stood by him through thick and thin and she deserved the little happiness he could give her. Fond as he was of his nephew, Hymie would just have to fend for himself.

What do you want? he growled at the customer sitting at the bar. The customer, an old friend and valued patron, looked up at Sam in surprise.

Hymie stood outside the tavern in a daze. It's getting late, he thought. I should get back. He stood in the fading sunlight and looked about. He looked at the sidewalk he was standing on. He looked at his car, his maroon Chevrolet. It was all so unreal. Some children ran by. The image of his dead brother suddenly came to mind. Nineteen years old and as blind as a bat, and yet they had taken him into the army. Did any of this have any meaning whatsoever? He wished he could weep, but he was beyond tears, beyond regret, beyond hope. He walked automatically to his car and got in. He looked back at Uncle Sam's tavern and snorted at his foolish daydreams.

I must be practical, he thought. Frieda and the children must be provided for. He did have some life insurance and there was a small bank account, but how long would that last? Who was there to turn to? Let's see. There was Tillie. No matter what the situation was she was not gonna let his wife and children die of starvation. And then there was Jack. Jack was devoted to his sister. And there was also Uncle Sam. He would certainly help out. Between the three of them...and there were some cousins as well. And weren't there some Jewish charity organizations a widow could apply to? He started the car, made several directional blunders, and finally found his way back to Fifty Bar and Grill. The place was beginning to fill up. He went behind the counter, took off his jacket and wrapped the coarse white apron about his waist.

Your wife called, Hymie, Phil said.

Thank you, said Hymie and he got busy serving beer and bantering with the customers. He just didn't have the heart to return Frieda's call. When the phone rang, ten minutes later, he let Phil answer it.

It's your wife.

Hymie walked reluctantly to the phone and picked it up.

Hello, he said.

So?

So, nothing.

He said nothing?

They're going to see a Broadway show tonight. A comedy.

How are you feeling?

Top of the world! I'm busy now.

What time will you be home?

I'll be home when I'll be home. He hung up and went back to work.

After the rush was over Adam took off his apron, hung it up and went over to Hymie. *I'm going upstairs for dinner*, he said. (Adam was eating with the Kopanskis now.) *What did your uncle have to say?*

He's going to see a Broadway show.

Adam said nothing, which Hymie was grateful for.

After Adam left Phil came over. *I can handle it now*, he said. (Tonight was Hymie's night off.)

That's all right, said Hymie.

Aren't you taking the night off?

You wanna take off?

Well, there are some things I could do, said Phil.

Go ahead.

You don't mind?

Since there was no reply Phil took off his apron and left. Hymie picked up the phone and dialed.

Hello, said Frieda.

I won't be home tonight. Phil had something to take care of.

Frieda sighed. It was dish night at the Hawthorne Avenue theatre and he could hear her disappointment.

You can go by yourself.

I'm not going to the movies by myself. You can't be that busy.

You can see through the phone? You know how busy I am?

Why are you like that? I try to be nice to you and all I get is a slap in the face. And she hung up.

He was trying to spare her the pain. Why couldn't she understand?

The place was empty. Hymie poured himself a double shot and downed it. As he set down the glass he happened to glance out the window. There he was, turning the corner, the man in the black suit with the goatee. He had a hell of a nerve! Fall had just barely begun. He had at least ten weeks to go. Why was he skulking about like that?

When Adam returned from dinner Hymie took him aside.

He was here again.

Who?

The man in the black suit.

Are you sure?

I'm positive.

Did he speak to you?

Hymie shook his head.

Then there's nothing to worry about. You're not the only one on his list, you know.

He's a busy man.

Is there anything wrong?

Is there anything wrong?! For an angel, Adam was really not that sensitive.

And then the angel's words echoed in his head. Hymie did have friends among his customers, and maybe, if they knew...

CHAPTER TEN

JOHNNY NOTTE

Hymie continued to work absent-mindedly. He regretted not going home. He regretted causing Frieda pain, but he just wasn't up to it. And when he was gone, she would probably resent him for deserting her. And his children would grow up hating him. Well, he wouldn't be there, so what difference did it make? He poured himself another double shot and then a customer insisted he join him in a beer. The immediacy of his predicament was becoming hazier and hazier. By the time Johnny Notte came into the place Hymie was feeling no pain.

How are you doin', Hymie? asked Johnny as they shook hands.

When did you get back?

This morning.

How was your vacation?

Fine. The weather was great. When you gonna paint this place? One of these days I'm gonna come in here and do it for you. Dottie says I spend more time here than I do at home, so I figure this place oughta look, at least, as good as my house.

The usual evening crowd began to gather. The shuffleboard game was started and Fifty Bar and Grill was warmed with laughter and talk. Someone slipped into the back room and started to play the piano. A few musical souls adjourned to the back room and for half an hour sang familiar songs at the top of their lungs. Hymie was determined to put his fears out of his mind, and there were moments when he was his old self again...a man at peace with the world, a man with unbounded love of humanity with a healthy sense of humor; a man who loved the world in spite of itself.

There were drinks on the house so often that Adam looked a little concerned. I mean even an angel knew that a man was in business to make money. By midnight the crowd had thinned out. Only Johnny Notte was left and two other men, deep in a drunken argument.

Hymie told Adam he could leave if he wanted to, since he did have to open up in the morning. Adam was reluctant to leave but Hymie insisted.

Adam hung up his apron, went into the back room and locked the door. He said his good nights and left through the swinging doors, and shortly after that the two customers departed, leaving Hymie alone with Johnny.

C'mon, Hymie, I'm buying you a good night drink, said Johnny and he sat down at one of the tables.

Hymie brought over a bottle and two glasses and joined his friend.

What do you know? They've promoted me to captain, said Johnny.

Before you know it they'll make you commissioner.

Thanks but no thanks. I'll stay right where I am.

You're still a detective?

You bet your ass I'm still a detective, with a nice little raise. And don't think I haven't forgotten the money I owe you, Hymie. Things are still a little tight right now, but if you ever need anything you just let me know. I owe you my life, buddy boy, and don't you forget it. Don't shrug your shoulders like that. If I hadn't had that operation I would have died. And if I hadn't had the money I wouldn't have had the operation.

You'd have gotten it somewhere.

Where? My brother? That son of a bitch! My sister? Huh! And that woman is loaded. But who came through for me? You, you bastard! I'd lay down my life for you, Hymie.

Don't say that again 'cause I might take you up on it.

What do you mean?

And Hymie launched into the story.

I believe in friendship, Hymie. Nobody ever says "dirty Jew" around me. To me all God's creatures are equal. Catholic, Jew or Protestant. They're all the same. But you've got the angels on your side, Hymie, so you've got nothing to worry about. How old's your mother?

I don't know. About seventy three.

She'll come through for you, kid. I know when my grandfather got to be that age, life wasn't much fun anymore. He couldn't wait to go. You know? I was just thinking. I'm around the City Hospital all the time, and some of the cases that come in there, you wouldn't believe. I'll keep my eyes open for you. I better be getting home.

And Johnny pulled out a five dollar bill, which Hymie tried to refuse.

No, no, no. I said the drinks were on me, said Johnny. *And I'm gonna start to pay you back. My first pay check as captain.*

Johnny got up from the table rather shakily and embraced Hymie rather clumsily. *Chin up, Buddy. You got Johnny Notte on your side. Have any of those punks ever hit you up for protection? You bet your ass they haven't, and they never will. Not as long as Johnny Notte's around. See you tomorrow, kid.*

Johnny slapped Hymie on the back and staggered out of the bar. The doors swung crazily behind him.

Hymie got up from the table, automaton-like, and took the bottle and the two glasses with him behind the bar. He placed the bottle on the shelf, rinsed out the glasses and looked about. Apparently Adam had done a good job cleaning up. One more drink. One final drink.

What the hell! It wasn't the end of the world. Three months could be a lifetime. Cast your bread upon the waters. Johnny wasn't the only friend he had, and he knew that Johnny would speak to others. Somehow, somewhere someone would come forward. He felt it in his bones. And if not...so what? He'd had his forty years. He would face death like a man.

He took off his apron, got into his jacket, set the alarm, locked the front door and walked to his car. You are the last, he thought, my old faithful Chevrolet. He got into the car, started off and wondered where the hell he was going.

He didn't want to go home. He just wasn't up to facing Frieda who, he was sure, was waiting up for him. The truth of the matter was, he felt guilty. It wasn't his fault but that didn't change things. He had given her two children and she would be left alone in the world, a neurotic woman with no idea of what it was like to earn a living. His was the easy part. He'd have nothing to worry about.

He found himself driving home automatically. On Frelingheysen Avenue Hymie came to Weequahic Park and turned left. He drove slowly, deep into the park and then stopped the car and got out.

It was cool, cool enough to wear a topcoat and yet it was just the beginning of September. A breeze rustled through the darkness. The leaves trembled. There was a moon, but not a very bright one.

Hymie walked up a hill, into a grove of trees. He didn't know where he was going or why. He wanted to commune with God, with someone or something. The trees reminded him of the battlefield where he had fought in the war. Maybe that was what it was all about. Life was a battle where no one ever really won. If one wasn't blown to bits one was eventually struck down in another way.

He thought of his two children. All the pain, all the agony Frieda had gone through to give them life. And for what? Hymie's head pounded with unanswered questions. He sat on the grass at the foot of a tree, leaned back and looked up at the sky. A star twinkled there in the distance, so calm, so undisturbed.

He woke with a start. The stars were gone. The sky was turning light blue. What time was it? He looked at his watch. After six. Where was he? Was he still in the army, bivouacked in the forest? He sat up and looked about. No guns. No soldiers. Just trees and grass.

He shivered with the cold, stood up and brushed the dirt from his clothes. He'd fallen asleep and spent the night there. What a state Frieda must be in by now! Maybe she'd telephoned the police. She'd done that once before, when he'd fallen asleep in the car on the way home and hadn't turned up in the morning.

He wandered about in circles until he found the road and there was his car. He was damp with dew and his bones felt stiff. He would probably come down with pneumonia, and that would be it. He got into the car and drove through the park.

How fresh and clean everything looked and smelled. And suddenly life was full of promise. The trees, the grass, the very road beneath the car seemed to throb with vitality. He drove through the familiar streets and, for some strange reason, his heart seemed to be at peace. He drove up Nye Avenue, passing Osborne Terrace, Schuyler Avenue, Goodwin Avenue and there was the house.

He made a U turn and parked in front of the house. Frieda was at the window. He walked quickly up the alley, through the back hall and up the three stairs into the kitchen. Frieda stood there, pale as a ghost. He waited for the angry words, the bitter denunciation, but she said nothing. She just stood there.

I'm sorry, he said.

Are you all right?

I took a ride in the park and I fell asleep. I'm sorry.

He came up to her and took her in his arms. He was surprised by the passion of her embrace. He kissed her and then led her into the bedroom, closing the door behind them.

The children will be getting up soon, she said, but offered no resistance.

After their love-making Frieda went to the bathroom. When she returned Hymie was fast asleep. She covered him with the light blanket and sat, studying his sleeping face in the dim light that broke through the sides of the drawn shades. She left the bedroom, closing the door behind her and went into the kitchen. She sat at the kitchen table and was soon lost in thought.

CHAPTER ELEVEN

JACK

The following Sunday Hymie and Frieda had planned to go to New York to visit her brother Jack and his wife, Molly, but Nathan had come down with a cold and now Rachel was sniffling and blowing as well, so they decided to postpone the trip for a week. Nothing was heard from Tillie so Frieda called her. Tillie was cool on the phone. Morris's operation was scheduled for the first of October. Meyer, their salesman, was going to be in downtown Newark during the week and he would drop off Adam's suit at "the place." And so he did.

Both Hymie and Adam were behind the bar when Meyer arrived. Hymie treated Meyer to a drink while Adam went into the back to try on the suit. It fitted perfectly and Adam got several whistles and catcalls from the customers. Hymie inquired about Tillie and Morris and the boys. Everyone was fine. Morris was apprehensive about the operation, but looking forward to it, since it might relieve the pain in his leg. Business was picking up at the clothing store. People were beginning to shop for the cold weather. Winter would soon be here. Hymie wondered whether Tillie had told Meyer about his predicament but assumed they hadn't since Meyer's inquiries were quite routine. After Meyer left Adam took the suit upstairs to his room, then relieved Hymie behind the bar and Hymie went home.

Since Hymie's night in the park something had happened between him and Frieda. A new understanding had sprung up. All their little differences, their major quarrels, the bitterness, the guilt...all the barriers between them seemed to have vanished. The respect and affection for one another that had been present during their courtship and the early days of their marriage had returned. Frieda bit her tongue when she felt a sharp word at the end of it and Hymie treated her little complaints and phobias with a tenderness that surprised them both. Even the children became aware of something special in the air. Something intangible. Something sad and beautiful and frightening.

Aunt Rose had called. She and Uncle Sam had wanted to take the children for a ride on Sunday but Frieda said they expected to go to New York. If there was a change in plans she would let her know. The week flew by quickly. The childrens' colds seemed under control and Saturday night Frieda phoned Molly to tell her they'd be coming out the next day.

Frieda was all keyed up about the visit. It hadn't always been that way, but now any event slightly out of the ordinary was enough to upset her equilibrium. The children, of course, were all excited. Hymie knew that Jack would have no answers and yet, one could never be sure. He did have something to say about everything. At any rate Jack would have to be informed about what was probably going to take place.

Hymie tried to sort out his feelings about his brother-in-law. In his own way Jack was just as neurotic as Frieda, maybe more so. Intellectually the man was brilliant, there was no doubt about that. Socially, in his relationship to other people that is, the man was stupid. There was no doubt about that. Jack went out of his way to insult everyone and everything. Man, woman and child, none were safe from his sarcasm. He could not address anyone without an implicit sneer. He sneered at the world. He sneered at himself. He mocked God for having placed him in an idiotic world, in an untenable position.

Actually Jack did have some talent as a writer. He'd written some articles which had been printed in the Jewish News, but he'd never pursued a career in journalism. This wasn't Poland. This was America, and he was intimidated by this barbaric country and insecure about his mastery of the English language. And besides, he'd had enough of poverty in Palestine where he'd been living for over a year. (One of his cronies there had been a young man named David Ben Gurion. Perhaps he should have stayed in Palestine and pursued a career in politics.)

He hated being a furrier. He had a terrible sinus condition which was aggravated by the fur. He had all sorts of undiagnosed illnesses, most of them stemming from his "nerves". He loved his little boy and was jealous of him as well. He hoped his son would be more successful in life than he was, and he was uneasy about the prospect that the child might actually put his father to shame. He quarreled with Molly incessantly and violently and most of their quarrels were about little Nathan. (The boy was also named after his and Frieda's deceased father.) Jack claimed, with some truth, that Molly spoiled the boy to death. Molly argued, with some truth, that Jack was concerned with nothing and no one but his own little problems.

As a rule Hymie did not look forward to visiting his brother-in-law's home. He usually came away with a headache. Everything there was so hectic. And, of course, the traffic in New York was not like the traffic in Newark. The lights were different. The rhythm was different. All in all, visiting Jack and Molly, was an unsettling experience.

In the back seat of the car Nathan and Rachel were cheerful and alert. In the front Frieda was tense, Hymie preoccupied. Jack, at various stages of his life kept flashing across his mind. Jack as a brilliant scholar in Poland. Jack, all eager and bright, arriving in America on the day that Nathan was born. Jack, during his bachelor days, showing up at their home for dinner, lost and confused. Jack at his wedding, nervous and morose. He was marrying Molly on the rebound. Minnie, Frieda's best friend and the girl with whom he'd been enamored, had been put off by Jack's arrogance and cynicism.

There was only one person in the world who was not an object of Jack's mockery, his twin soul, Frieda. Perhaps it was their harrowing war experiences that had brought about their deep understanding of one another. During the war they had been father and mother to their younger brothers and sisters, when their parents had sent them to Prague, to shelter them from the approaching enemy. That winter in the city had been a nightmare and had left an indelible impression on both the brother and the sister. Hunger and cold are things one never forgets.

Hymie made several wrong turns. It had been some time since their last visit to the Bronx and there was always something different to contend with.

There was a long wait at the Holland Tunnel, even longer than usual and Nathan kept popping his bubble gum. Coming out of the tunnel the road was under construction and Hymie had to take an alternate route.

For a while they found themselves heading for Brooklyn. Hymie heaved a sigh of relief when they hit the Grand Concourse. They rode in the shadow of the elevated tracks which rumbled and rattled and clanged overhead. Everything was so much noisier. Hymie was glad he had settled in Newark, and that set him thinking about the quirks of fate. He had settled in Newark because Uncle Sam had offered him a job. Suppose he had settled in New York? Would his life have been any different? Perhaps the man in the black suit with the goatee wouldn't have been able to find him in that concrete jungle.

I want to go to the bathroom, piped Rachel.

I told you to go before we left, said Frieda.

I did, but I have to go again.

All right, all right. We'll be there soon.

The neighborhood was beginning to look familiar. There was the kosher delicatessen and there was the bakery. East Two Hundred and Eighth Street.

Hymie turned right and drove up the steep hill. He drove carefully around the strangely twisting corners. There was the synagogue and there were the apartment buildings, one next to the other. Not very

conducive to gracious living. The buildings weren't old and yet they
looked like they'd been there forever. The graffiti on the walls didn't
help. No, Hymie was glad he'd settled in Newark. As the four of them
piled out of the Chevrolet a cloud concealed the sun and the weather took
a rather ominous turn. Was it going to rain?

There was Jack standing in front of his building, the shoes that
always looked too big, the dark suit that never quite fit, the pencil
mustache and the wavy hair combed straight back. He was fidgeting
nervously as he watched his relatives approach him from across the
street.

So...you're here, he muttered. Jack had a stammer. Sometimes
it felt as if the words were being dredged up from the very soul of his
being and filtered through some raw wound. And always that wry irony.

Hello, Jack, said Frieda and she kissed her brother.

Who...are these people you brought with you?

Hello, Uncle Jack, said Nathan and he shook his uncle's hand.

Doesn't...she know her Uncle Jack? said Jack to his sister,
referring slyly to Rachel.

Hello, Uncle Jack, said Rachel shyly and stood on her toes to
kiss him.

She has to go to the bathroom, said Frieda.

So...take her upstairs.

Is Molly there?

She stepped out for a minute.

She went to the store?

*What store? She's with her...mother, where she always is. I don't
know what...she's...gonna do if we...move.*

You moving?

Who knows?

I'll take her upstairs. Is the door open?

*It's open, it's open. Take her upstairs already. We don't want an
accident.*

Frieda took Rachel by the hand and led her into the building.

So how are you, Hymie? You selling... a lot of beer?

All right?

*What...does that mean? All right. You're feeling all right?
Business is g-good? What does that...mean, all right?*

I'm feeling all right and business is good.

*So...there you are. T-top of the world. You're a successful
business man. The world is your...oyster. And your...boy is getting big.
He'll be bar-mitzvahed soon and...that's gonna...cost you a fortune. All*

right, so...that's what it's for. You...can't take it with you. He doesn't...look like you. He...looks like Frieda. All right. So, that's how it is. You...found your way all right?

I'm here.

So that's how it is. You're here. I'm here and I feel like hell.

What's the matter?

If...I knew what was the matter I'd be fine. They have...medicine these days for everything. The only...trouble is, the doctors...don't know what medicine to give me. That's all right, too. All...good things must come to an end. You want...to go upstairs or you want...to stay down here?

It's a beautiful day.

For you it's...a beautiful day. For me...it's another...miserable Sunday. All right, all right. So let's...stay down here. You wanna...go for a walk? That's the only pleasure I get. I walk. I walk for miles. You look a little pale. You could...use some exercise.

Tell your mother we're going for a walk, Hymie said to Nathan.

You know which apartment is...mine? Uncle Jack asked Nathan.

Nathan nodded, hesitated for a moment then entered the building.

He's...a nice looking boy. All right. So...he'll grow up and ...get married and...that'll be that.

The two men started to walk slowly around the corner and down the hill. There was nothing but large apartment buildings on either side of the street. No trees. No grass. Cement wherever you looked.

Jack stopped in front of one of the buildings. *I'd better let Molly know you're here, otherwise she'll spend the rest of the day there. Y-You don't want to come in...do you?*

Hymie shrugged.

Th-they'll...talk your ear off. I'll be right out. Jack crossed the street and entered one of the apartment buildings.

Hymie stood waiting on the sidewalk. He was getting a headache already, but he was glad he'd have Jack to himself.

Molly said I...should have brought you in, said Jack on his return. *Th-they'll come up to the apartment and we won't be able ...to get rid of them. She should have married her...mother, not me. I've never seen...a grown woman so...attached to her mother. Her mother...and the boy. All right, that's another story. She's...killing that boy. Sh-she doesn't...let him breathe. If he coughs, right away she's on the phone with the doctor. She used...to bring him to the doctor every day until...he told her to stop bothering him. You're very...talkative. I can't get a word in edgewise.*

You're doing all right.

So what was the matter with you?

I was sick.

I...know you were sick.

I'm not sure.

Wh-what did the doctor say/

The flu. My stomach. Did Frieda tell you?

She told Molly. You're seeing angels.

I've got to find someone to take my place.

*C-c-come on, Hymie? Wh-what do you take me for? A fool? This
is the...twentieth century. N-nobody sees angels anymore, except...maybe
in the crazy house.*

He's working for me.

Who?

*This angel. His name is Adam. And he's the one that made the
bargain for me. Otherwise I wouldn't be here right now.*

Wh-what bargain? Wh-what are you talking about?

I thought Frieda told you.

*Hymie, I...think you need a rest, a long...rest. I'm...surprised at
you. I thought you were a sensible man.*

I'll introduce you to him

You'll introduce me...to an angel?

He's here on earth.

*Oh, c-come on, Hymie. All right, sometimes when you're sick you
see all...sorts of things. You had a fever.*

I didn't have any fever.

All right. Have it your way.

I was hoping... I mean, you're an educated man.

*Hymie, the s-scholars themselves, the most orthodox
rabbis...have grave doubts about the existence of angels. But you see
angels. If you knew...anything about Jewish theology you wouldn't be
telling me all this...nonsense. You had a bad dream.*

You don't believe me.

*I believe that you...believe. The human mind is capable of
anything from a...statue by Michelangelo to a...Genghis...Kahn. I have
an imagination...that I can't control. Th-that's my sickness. My...mind
goes everywhere. It...sees everything. I can't stop it. Unfortunately...my
flesh is here in the Bronx, on Two Hundred and Eighth Street, or on
Seventh Avenue in a sweat shop, cutting fur. F-frieda...has the same
sickness. My little Nathan has it, too. I can see it already. And I*

think...maybe your Nathan has it, too, from his mother. B-but you.
You're a sensible man, Hymie. P-please.

You have no suggestions?

Sure, I have a suggestion. G-go see a...psychiatrist. I don't
believe in them, but...maybe they can help you.

You went to one once. Did he help you?

He...gave me a lot of...bullshit. But maybe for...somebody else...

The two men came to Mosholu Park. The elevated train rumbled
in the distance. Children were playing on the grass, running about the
paths. Adults were sitting on the benches or walking leisurely. The sun
kept peeking out from behind the clouds and then disappearing again.

All right, said Hymie, *If you have such a good imagination,*
imagine what I'm telling you is true. What would you do in my position?

I'd take a couple of...aspirins and forget about it. C-come on.
Don't talk nonsense!

Hymie saw it was useless. Jack would not accept his story and
that was that. It had never occurred to Hymie that Jack would doubt him.
No one had up until now. Could it possibly be a bad dream? But there
was Adam. Or maybe Adam really was just a bum off the street. Since
the depression there were all sorts of men, penniless and footloose,
wandering about. Well educated men. Intelligent men.

Earthbound and practical. That's the way his brother-in-law saw
him. A dreamer. Full of imagination. That's the way Hymie had always
thought of Jack. And now, was it possible? Were their roles reversed?

So...what are you thinking? asked Jack.

I don't know what to think.

Take my advice. F-forget it. Do...you know how this is upsetting
Frija? I'm surprised at you, Hymie.

What are you surprised? You're the only one that can be
nervous? You and Frija?

So...there you...are. You said it yourself. It's your...nerves.
You've been...through a war. Your brother was killed...right in front of
you.

Naturally, it's my nerves. If you had less than three months to
live, how would you feel?

Grateful. Every night I go to bed I pray I won't wake up.

I'll do you a favor. I'll answer your prayers. You can take my
place.

Look, I'm not...gonna play this game with you. I...don't want to
talk about it anymore. It's nonsense!

The two men walked on in silence. Finally, as they passed a bench, Jack made towards it and sat down. Hymie followed suit.

I'm serious. I think you ought to...see a psychiatrist, Jack said. Hymie said nothing.

Whatever you do...please don't talk to Frija about this anymore. If you...want a healthy wife. You hear me?

I hear you.

Sometimes I think...there's a c-curse on this family. He sighed. *We're born to die, Hymie, and it'll come...soon enough.* And he patted Hymie on the shoulder.

Hymie looked up in surprise. It was the first time Jack had ever expressed any warmth towards anyone except his sister.

I'm very disappointed in you, Hymie. V-very disappointed. You were one of...the few people I thought I could depend on. If you should have a...breakdown, G-god forbid, what would happen to Frija? This is very selfish, of you.

Hymie sighed and looked up at Jack. His brother-in-law sat forlornly, his shoulders bent forward. His eyes were moist and his brow furrowed.

Don't worry, Hymie said. *I'll get over it.*

Tears flooded Jack's eyes and he took out a handkerchief and wiped them. Hymie sat there alarmed, not knowing what to do. Jack was nothing, if not unpredictable. Where was the oratory? Where was the invective? Where was the bitter sarcasm? It was embarrassing to see the man weep. Whom was he weeping for? It wasn't for his brother-in-law, you could be sure of that. Was it for his sister and the possible predicament she might find herself in? Or was the man weeping for himself and the prospect of an additional burden...an additional burden added to the burden he found impossible to bear?

Finally Jack blew his nose, put his handkerchief away and rose. *All right.* he said. *We've...talked enough. We...better be getting back.* He took a little bottle from his jacket pocket, opened it, took out a white pill and popped it into his mouth. He screwed back the cap and put the bottle into his pocket.

What's that? Hymie asked.

It's a pill...for my sinus. Th-that's what I live on, pills. I'll show you a medicine cabinet full of...pills. Pinks ones and...green ones and...red ones and yellow ones and...blue ones. Th-this is a white one. And you think they do me any good?

So why do you take them?

I keep hoping. M-maybe they do relieve me...a little. I've got to get out of the...fur business. It's...killing me. It's no...joke. Every day...I go in there...I die.

So what would you do?

I don't know. Maybe a...business of my own. Molly's brother...is opening a m-market. A grocery store.

You mean you'd go partners?

P-partners? We'd...kill each other in a...week. I've got to be my own boss. I don't know. I'll...look around.

Jack and Hymie walked slowly back to the apartment building. When they arrived at the entrance Jack said, *You think I...wanna go up there? It's like a prison.*

You're not gonna go up?

I'll come up, I'll...come up.

Jack sighed, entered the building and walked slowly up the stairs. Hymie followed him. The apartment was at the head of the first landing. The door was ajar. Apartment 1 B. Jack pushed the door open and ushered Hymie in.

Jack? came Molly's voice from the kitchen.

No. It's President Roosevelt.

Molly came into the room. *I'm telling you. You have guests and you disappear.*

That's all right, said Frieda, who was standing in the living room.

I took Hymie for a walk. I showed him...the...Bronx. So, how...do you like the...Bronx? You wanna move here?

No thanks, said Hymie.

I don't...blame you, said Jack. *I'd like to get out of here myself.*

So where would you go? asked Molly.

Anywhere...but here. It's a jungle.

A jungle? A jungle! You talk nonsense.

Everything I say...is nonsense.

You said it, not me. Hello, Hymie. Molly kissed Hymie. *You're looking well. And the children, Gott sei danke, they're beautiful.*

B-beautiful, shmootiful. As along as they're healthy. Are they healthy? Jack asked Frieda.

'Gott sei dank', she said.

So...there you...are. Some...body in the family is...healthy.

And what's the matter with you? asked Frieda.

If you...have a...whole week, I'll tell you.

There's nothing wrong with him, said Molly.

You know there's nothing wrong with me!

I'm just repeating what the doctors said.

The doctors! The doctors! What do they know? Money, that's all they know.

If they don't know anything, why do you go to them?

I'm...guinea pig, for...science. Th-they practice up on me.

Oh, come on, Jack. How many doctors have you been to? And what do they all say?

I know how I feel. I'm sick.

You're sick in the head. That's where you're sick.

And you think that's not a sickness? That's...the worst kind of...sickness.

So go back to your psychiatrist. He went to a psychiatrist, you know.

So what did he say? asked Frieda.

He kicked him out of the office he made such a fuss. He was gonna call the police. He kept telling the psychiatrist that he was the one that was crazy.

He was...crazy all right. Crazy like a fox, that...phoney.

Everyone's a phoney, by you. You're the phoney.

I'm a monster, not a phoney, snapped Jack and he walked through the living room into the bathroom, slamming the door behind him.

I don't know what's gonna become of him, said Molly. *He's got a bathroom full of pills and that's what he lives on. I could tell you stories, but what's the use?*

You don't have to tell me. It's a curse.

I'm nervous myself, said Molly. *But the way he carries on, you'd think he was the only one in the world. I don't know where it's going to end. So let's eat. I'm sorry I didn't have a chance to prepare anything. You'll have to excuse me.*

We didn't come here to eat, said Frieda.

I opened some tuna fish. You like tuna fish, Hymie?

Tuna fish is fine.

So let's go into the kitchen. We'll eat first. The kitchen's so small. And then I'll feed the children.

You didn't put onions in the tuna fish, I hope, said Frieda.

No, no, I know. Onions disagree with you.

I like onions, but they don't like me. Unless they're cooked.

Jack came back into the living room.

Are you gonna eat, Jack? Molly asked.

So I'll eat.

You like tuna fish.

When...I can't get steak, I'll eat tuna fish.

I feel terrible. You always have such a nice meal when we come out there. But you didn't know whether you were coming or not.

That's some excuse, said Jack. *If...they changed their mind... the food would have gone to waste?*

Usually I have something in the house.

If you didn't spend so...much time with your mother...

Jack, please, said Frieda. *I didn't come here to hear you fight. Tuna fish is fine.*

The four of them filed into the little kitchen flooded with sunlight.

If I'd known a couple of days in advance... It just so happens we have an excellent butcher now. He opened a few months ago. If that sun is too much for you, Hymie, just pull down the shade.

Hymie lowered the shade as he sat down next to the window at the little round table.

Your kitchen is very light, said Frieda.

We're lucky. We happen to be on the right side of the building. Usually a back apartment you don't get much light. Molly set out the food. *I got fresh rolls. We have a very good bakery.*

I know, said Frieda. *I must remember to pick up some bread on the way home.*

Help yourself, Hymie, said Molly.

Frieda took a plate and filled it for Hymie. *You have some butter?* she asked.

I'm sorry, said Molly and produced the butter.

These rolls are very good, said Frieda. *Why don't you have a roll, Jack?*

No rolls!

He can't chew, because of his teeth. I tell him to go to the dentist. You think he listens to me?

That man is a crook.

So go to another dentist. They're all crooks, continued Molly, anticipating Jack. *Did you ever hear such a thing? This is the way it is all the time.*

When his teeth get bad enough, he'll go, said Frieda.

He won't go. He likes to suffer. He's up all night, sometimes, because of the pain.

So why don't you go, Jack? asked Frieda.

I'll g-go...when I g-go.

It's no use talking to him.

You're so brave. You...were supposed to go to the doctor weeks ago. Did...you go?

I have a wart I need burned off. I've been putting it off, said Molly.

So I'm not the...only c-coward.

But my wart doesn't keep me up all night.

All right. So that's it. You aren't happy unless...you nag me. Go...nag your mother.

She's telling you for your own good, said Frieda. *Why are you so stubborn? Don't you want to feel better?*

Wh-hen I'm dead I'll feel better.

What kind of talk is that? Frieda asked.

That's the way he talks all the time. He hasn't got a friend in the world. No one comes up here anymore. He insults everybody. I used to have all sorts of friends.

Some friends!

Why are you like that? Frieda asked.

Because I don't believe in being phoney. I tell people the truth.

There are ways of telling the truth. And what happens when people tell you the truth? You don't like it anymore than they do. One of these days you're gonna tell the wrong person the truth and you're gonna end up in the hospital. He got into a fight with the super the other day, who happens to be a very nice man. The window in the bedroom needs a new cord. The super said he would fix it on Monday or Tuesday. He's got to lot to do. Yesterday Jack goes down there and gives him an argument. The man came up here afterwards and said to me, "Mrs. Tall, keep that husband of yours away from me, because I'm gonna punch him in the nose." And he's not the only one. My brother-in-law, Moe, Sarah's husband, he doesn't come up here anymore.

He can go to hell!

Everybody can go to hell.

Right!

Is that the way to live? Without a friend in the world? He doesn't need people. He goes for a walk and he walks. I like to have people to talk to. I like to have friends.

S-so who's stopping you?

You are. Nobody will come up here anymore.

So go there. I don't want all those bums in my house.

Everybody's a bum by you.

Molly's right, said Frieda. *You can't live without people.*

You can't live without people. Molly can't live without people. I...can live very happily without people.

But you're not happy. You're miserable. Molly turned to Frieda. *I don't know what I'm gonna do.*

Your mother comes here, doesn't she? That's all you need.

Come on, Jack, said Frieda.

C-come on, c-come on. What do you know. Are you here? She has the whole neighborhood sorry for her. P-poor Molly. She has to...live with that...bum. She nags the life out of me.

When do I nag you? Molly turned to Frieda. *I have to tell him to take a bath. I have to tell him to change his underwear. That's what he calls nagging.*

Too many baths is un...healthy.

Once a week is not too many.

All...right. We're eating dinner now. They don't want to hear about underwear.

Hymie started to rise.

Would you like some coffee, Hymie? asked Molly.

We're not coffee drinkers, said Frieda.

Maybe a glass of milk? I have plenty of milk.

If you have some soda, I'll take a little, said Hymie.

I have some Coke.

That's fine.

Hymie drank the Coke Molly poured for him, excused himself and edged out of the kitchen into the living room. The talk was aggravating his headache and the smallness of the kitchen was giving him claustrophobia.

He looked about the living room. Two large books cases with glass doors. The end tables with candy dishes and tiny ash trays. The picture on the wall over the sofa, a rural country side scene. He studied the photograph over the book case. There was Jack as a young man, wearing an Arab robe and turban, surrounded by several swarthy Arabs. A few years ago Jack was quite a dashing figure. What happened to all that mystery? What happened to all that romance?

Hymie walked into the bedroom on the right. He could hear the children's voices. There were the three of them, sitting on the floor...Nathan, Rachel and little Nathan, playing with one of little Nathan's games. The little boy rose dutifully and approached his uncle. Hymie bent over and little Nathan kissed him.

Hello, Uncle Hymie, he said.

Hymie picked the boy up and held him in his arms. *How are you?*

I'm f-fine.

What are you doing?

We're p-playing a...racing game. My Aunt Sarah gave it to me.

Hymie studied the boy's plump face, the scar over the right eye, the ruddy cheeks, the watery blue eyes. What lay in store for the child? How would he emerge from this strife-torn home? Hymie set the boy down and the children resumed their game. He went into the bathroom to relieve himself. The apartment was certainly neat enough, and clean. He returned to the living room to find Jack sitting in the easy chair next to the window.

So...you have to waste a Sunday, coming to the Bronx.

It's not wasted.

How's Tillie doing?

Fine. Morris is having an operation this week, on his leg.

Is it serious?

The doctors say it will help him walk better.

Tillie's the one. If...I had her guts I'd be all right.

Molly walked through the living room to the bedroom to bring the children in for their dinner. As she returned with the children in tow she said to Jack, *Maybe you want to take Hymie for a walk.*

We took a walk already. You complained.

I just thought you might wanna get some air. It's a beautiful day.

There's plenty of air here by the window.

Do as you please, said Molly and followed the children into the kitchen.

So...that's how it is, said Jack and sighed. He looked out the window, jiggling his feet nervously.

Hymie had the feeling that his bother-in-law wanted to be out there somewhere, walking alone and brooding his morbid thoughts. When the children finished their meal they went back to the bedroom and Frieda joined the two men in the living room.

It's a nice apartment, said Frieda.

The old apartment...was just as nice.

But you needed another room for the boy.

What room?! He sleeps in the same room with Molly.

And where do you sleep?

In the other room. You...don't believe me when I tell you. He wakes up at night. He has bad dreams. She...has to be there. If I get out of bed and move around, she says...that I'll wake him, so I sleep in the other room.

That's not right, said Frieda.

What...are you talking about? It's the romance of the century.

The doorbell rang. The half open door swung open and Molly's mother came in. She was a full bodied woman of medium height, like Molly, but heavier and she wore the traditional wig that Jewish women wore in the old country. She came into the living room and shook hands with Frieda and Hymie. *So, how are you?* she asked. The visitors answered politely and sat down again.

Jack treated his mother-in-law with respectful sarcasm. There was even a bit of affection in his tone towards her.

Molly came out of the kitchen with a bowl of fruit, which she placed on the coffee table in front of the sofa. *Help yourself,* she said.

The conversation turned toward the coming holiday. The women discussed food and clothes. Jack made several scathing remarks about the hypocrisy of religion. It was an opiate, a sham, a refuge for scoundrels and bums. Molly's mother listened patiently to the familiar tirade and treated Jack like some deranged child one had to indulge. Jack warmed to the subject, quoting freely from the Bible and other religious texts, some of them quite obscure. He spoke eloquently and at length. At times his face would grow flushed. At times he stammered, but the words tumbled out, impelled by some desperate need to be heard and understood. His knowledge seemed vast and unchallengeable. He spoke like an oracle and one could do nothing but greet the torrent of words with admiration, though some of the admiration was grudging.

They were joined by a neighboring couple whom Jack promptly proceeded to insult. The first insults were greeted with a shrug, but as they continued the woman grew icy and stiff and the man belligerent. For a moment it looked like the man was going to attack Jack. Between them, Frieda and Molly were able to change the subject and the confrontation, for all intensive purposes, was forgotten. The couple stayed on for a little while longer and as they rose to leave the man said, *Jack, you are a son of a bitch.*

And...what you are, said Jack, *I can't say in polite society, but...it's something that a woman has between her legs.*

Molly saw the couple out with apologies then turned to her guests and said, *You see? You see what he's like? I don't have to tell you.*

And you don't have to apologize for me either. I...don't want that son of a bitch in my house anymore.

Don't worry. They won't be here.

She's... as fat as a cow, and she used to be so pretty. I told her for her own good.

When you're perfect, you can criticize other people. I don't know what I'm gonna do.

You're mother's right here. Ask...her what you should do. said Jack and stalked out of the living room into the rear of the apartment.

Frieda rose and followed her brother. They could be heard arguing. Then their voices grew calmer and quieter.

I'm sorry, Hymie, said Molly. *What can I say?*

You don't have to say anything.

He ought to go back to that psychiatrist, said Molly's mother.

He wouldn't take him back, said Molly.

Well, he ought to do something, because one of these days someone's going to kill that man, said Molly's mother.

Maybe that's what he wants.

Frieda returned to the living room and looked toward Hymie. *We'd better start out. It'll be dark soon.*

I was gonna make some coffee. I bought a cake. It'll only take a minute.

You want come coffee? Frieda asked Hymie.

So let's have coffee.

Frieda shot a murderous glance at her husband, but there was no help for it now. Molly went into the kitchen to prepare the coffee. Molly's mother excused herself and left.

You can't have coffee at home?

Hymie shrugged and said nothing. There was no figuring the woman out. She can't wait to see her brother and now she's in a hurry. And besides, she asked him, didn't she?

The coffee and cake were consumed. The children had milk. The good-byes were said and said and said. Frieda, Hymie and the children finally descended the stairs, accompanied by Jack. He'd rejoined them for the coffee.

At the car Frieda turned to Jack and said, *Please Jack, for my sake, don't act like that.*

All...right. So that's how it is.

Frieda kissed her brother. Rachel kissed her uncle and Nathan shook hands with him and they got into the car.

So behave yourself, Jack said to Hymie. *You hear me? You know what I'm talking about.*

Hymie nodded and shook hands with his brother-in-law. *Good-bye, Jack.*

Jack watched Hymie get into the car, a disturbed and anxious expression on his face. *And...don't do anything foolish.*

Hymie nodded again, sighed and drove off. Jack stood on the curb watching, with grave concern, the car disappear.

The drive back to Newark was relatively peaceful, compared to the earlier part of the day. The children sat so quietly in the back of the car that Hymie looked back once to make sure they were all right. As they left the Bronx and came onto the West Side Highway Nathan broke the silence.

Where did Nathan get that scar over his eye?

He fell off a bicycle, Frieda answered. She said nothing about the epic quarrel of recrimination and guilt that had taken place between Jack and Molly concerning that fall. Jack had bought the tricycle for the boy, against Molly's wishes, and Molly held him responsible for the accident.

The sky over the Hudson River was salmon colored and blue. A cool breeze flowed through the car as they sped along the highway and Hymie's mind was filled with his brother-in-law. How painful life was for Jack, and how hopeless. It's true that Hymie's situation was desperate, but at least there was some glimmer of hope. If angels walked the earth and Death was a man, certainly a miracle was not unthinkable. But Jack's life was...impossible.

It grew darker and the lights began to twinkle across the river in New Jersey. It was quite dark by time the Benders arrived home. After a light supper they listened to the radio for a while. Nathan did some homework. Rachel worked on her coloring book. Frieda darned some socks and mended some clothes while Hymie read the paper. He went to bed early, mentally and emotionally exhausted.

CHAPTER TWELVE

THE LETTER

The next day Hymie told Adam about the visit to New York. *He doesn't believe in angels,* Hymie said.

Adam looked thoughtful for a moment and then said quietly, *There are many dead men walking the earth who haven't been buried yet.* And the angel continued his task of rinsing out some glasses.

October came in brisk and cool. It was the most beautiful Autumn that Hymie could remember. All the way down Nye Avenue the trees were a riot of color...red, brown, yellow and orange. The air was so fresh and invigorating. It was as if all of Newark had been turned into a park.

Hymie, Frieda and the children rose in the morning full of energy to face the day, laden with promise. Everything was going so well, both at home and in "the place". Business had never been better and Hymie and his wife had never lived so compatibly.

Financial insecurity had played a great part in the friction between husband and wife. Frieda accused Hymie of being too cavalier with the money he made. Now, for the first time, Hymie began to count pennies. If, God forbid, Frieda was to be left alone in the world he had to try to pile up some extra cash. He must see to it that "the place" yielded as much as possible. No more rounds on the house. He even cut down on his own little nips. No more little loans to needy customers. Hymie had always been an easy mark for every charity, every collection. Not anymore. He hated himself for doing it, but he became stingy. Painful as it was his first obligation was to his own flesh and blood.

He hated even to spend the money for the seats in the synagogue for Rosh Hashonah. The price of the seats had gone up considerably and, for the first time, he felt that he had to buy a seat for Nathan. The boy just couldn't squeeze in anymore. He was twelve years old and, in less than a year, he would be Bar Mitzvahed. (If I live that long)

That week Morris had his operation and came through it fine. Hymie and Frieda visited him in the hospital one afternoon and he seemed to be in pretty good spirits.

The Sunday following the visit to New York Uncle Sam and Aunt Rose picked up Nathan and Rachel and took them for a ride and then to dinner in a nice restaurant. Hymie and Frieda spent the afternoon

147

visiting some cousins. It felt strange calling on people without the children.

The following evening the holiday began. It had been raining a good part of the day and as Hymie and Nathan walked to the synagogue the smell of decaying leaves filled the air.

Hymie's thoughts were redolent with death. Every cemetery he had seen, every grave he had visited passed before his eyes. Perhaps there was something really beautiful about death, after all. The memory of his father and his brother was just a faint, gentle haze. Their suffering, whatever it had consisted of, had been, after all, but a brief moment in time. How easily we make room for death and how commonplace it really is.

He thought about his mother's letter and wondered what her answer would be. Could he accept her offer, if she were to make it? Tillie would never forgive him, nor would his other siblings perhaps. But what about his wife and his children?

The synagogue was only a block and a half from the Bender home, up Nye Avenue, past Wolcott Terrace to Clinton Place and there, just off the corner of Clinton Place and Nye Avenue was the red brick building that housed the Congregation of Agudath Israel.

A thought suddenly occurred to Hymie. He had no plot. Jack Goldfarb was in charge of the cemetery and he'd been after Hymie for quite some time to buy a family plot. *You'd better get one now,* he'd said. *Prices are going up.*

No, Hymie said to himself, that I will not do. Maybe I'm superstitious, but I will not buy a plot! It would just be inviting disaster.

On the eve of Rosh Hashanah the father and son rounded the corner, which was an empty lot surrounded by a large wire fence...the ground owned by the congregation...and they walked up the brick stairs into the synagogue. The service had just begun.

Hymie hadn't bothered to bring his own prayer shawl. He picked one up from the table in the lobby and handed one to Nathan. Skull caps on their heads Hymie and Nathan entered the synagogue and took seats toward the rear. No one bothered to take their regular seats since it was never that crowded on the evening before the New Year holiday. Hymie muttered a blessing, kissed the prayer shawl, wrapped it around his shoulders and Nathan followed suit. Hymie then took a prayer book from the little shelf on the back of the bench in front of him and handed one to Nathan. He found the place for the boy, opened his own book and, joining the service, began to mumble his prayers.

Nathan watched his father out of the corner of his eye. The boy had been having strange misgivings of late. He'd begun to wonder why he was praying. He'd even begun to question the dignity of prayer. Why should a man beg for favors? Well, wasn't that what they were doing? Begging for favors? And why should anyone be entitled to any special consideration from God? Shouldn't ones actions speak for themselves? And, as far as praising God was concerned, if there really was a God, was the Almighty that insecure that he needed all this flattery?

Nathan had said nothing about all this to his father. Things like that were never discussed. He might, one day, speak to his mother about his doubts, but as far as his father was concerned, they'd never had any sort of a conversation to speak of anyway. He'd begun to think of himself as an individual, apart from the family and, standing next to this man who'd given him life, he felt like a stranger.

And then Nathan remembered Adam. He was the one to talk to, if he really was an angel, and, of course, he was. But how forthcoming would Adam be? Maybe there were things that human beings were not supposed to know and Adam, in his own gentle way, was rather reticent. Well, if the opportunity ever arose, he would certainly have some questions to ask this...stranger.

The synagogue was a little more crowded than it was on the Sabbath, but not nearly as full as it would be the following day. Hymie nodded greetings to several familiar faces. The prayers he was saying, the holiday, the evening itself was taking on a very special significance. He listened, in rapt silence, to the golden voice of the new cantor. That was the reason the price of the seats had gone up. But he was worth it. What a voice! He was being serenaded to heaven in style. Or was it hell? But we don't believe in hell. Or do we?

After the service Hymie shook hands with several of the men and bits of gossip were exchanged. Mr. Rosenfeld had died of a heart attack a few weeks ago. Goldfarb's son was getting married next month. There was talk of the congregation selling the building and moving to a new location.

Hymie and Nathan left the group of men, walked down the brick stairs and across Clinton Place to Nye Avenue. The brisk, damp air was refreshing after the stuffiness of the synagogue. There was an awkward silence between father and son.

Finally Nathan said, *The cantor was very good.*

Hymie muttered his agreement. Why was it so difficult for him to talk to his son? What was this barrier that existed between them?

It was evening now. A bright, starry night. The man and boy skirted the puddles as they walked down Nye avenue. Hymie studied his son and wondered whether he ought to confide in him. After all the boy would have to assume some responsibilities when he was gone. But Frieda was so insistent on protecting the children. *They'll have enough to worry about when they grow up,* she insisted. *Why shouldn't they have the childhood that we didn't have?*

When they reached the house they walked up the front stairs rather than through the back. This was, after all, a holiday.

The table in the dining room was all set. Frieda and Rachel came to greet them. Frieda wore her navy blue dress and had put on some earrings. Hymie felt a pang at the beauty of his wife and he marveled at how lucky he was. The little family kissed one another.

Good yom tov! Good yom tov!

How was the new "chazan"? asked Frieda.

Fine, said Hymie.

He was excellent, said Nathan. *He sounds like an opera singer.*

He is, said Hymie. *He sings opera.*

So let's eat, said Frieda.

Hymie looked meaningfully at Frieda and she took the hint. It was a holiday, after all, and she produced the liquor. She even joined Hymie in a drink. Nathan was allowed a small one as well, and even Rachel was indulged with a sip. Then there was a piece of challah dipped in honey to insure a sweet new year and dinner (referred to as supper) was served. A full, elaborate meal with all sorts of delicacies and surprises. There was even a special desert, that tart "parve" apple pie, baked only for special occasions.

The meal was finished rather late in the evening and by the time the dishes were put away it was almost time for bed. The children were allowed to listen to the radio for a short while and then were hustled off.

Hymie and Frieda sat in the front for a while. They could see the lights in the houses across the street.

Do you always have to bury yourself in that paper? Frieda asked.

So what do you want me to do?

Talk to me for a while.

So what do you want to talk about?

Hymie folded the paper and put it aside. Frieda found all sorts of things to discuss. Sometimes the conversation verged on an argument, but even then it was amiable and gentle. I'm really a happy man, thought Hymie. If I'm to die in a couple of months, at least I can say I was happy for a little while. They went to bed early. It took Hymie a long time to fall asleep but when he did doze off he slept soundly.

Frieda let him sleep as long as possible and he had to rush to get ready for the synagogue. No breakfast was to be eaten before the service anyway. The children, however, were allowed some coffee and a small piece of the apple pie.

Rachel was left upstairs under the care of Mrs. Newman and Frieda, Hymie and Nathan started out the door. As Frieda locked the front door Hymie and Nathan stood waiting on the porch. The mailman came up the stairs with his bag.

Got some mail for you, Mr. Bender, he said and handed Hymie a couple of envelopes, then departed.

One of the envelopes contained the phone bill. The other was a light weight airmail letter from Europe with his mother's familiar awkward printing of his English name and address.

What is it? Frieda asked.

Hymie handed her the envelopes. She looked at them then at Hymie. *I'll put them in the mail box*, she said and went back into the hall.

Was that a letter from Europe? Nathan asked.

Yes, said Frieda.

Aren't you gonna open it?

It's Rosh Hashanah. We'll open it tomorrow.

Suppose it's something important?

Whatever it is, it can wait one day.

Nathan just couldn't keep up with all these fine distinctions regarding what one could or could not do. Hymie said nothing. He'd just as soon postpone the momentous event.

Hymie and Frieda remained in the synagogue all morning, without leaving it once. They were, as a rule, very earnest about their prayers, and this Rosh Hashanah they prayed even harder.

Nathan sat next to his father and looked longingly out the open window. Hymie was also anxious for the morning to pass but he tried not to show it. After all, he still had another day and a half...another day and a half before he could read his mother's letter.

The morning dragged on and finally... it was almost two o'clock...the service came to an end. That new "chazan" certainly liked to drag things out.

Rachel had been brought to the synagogue by her brother, late in the morning, and she'd remained in the women's section, with her mother, until the end of the service.

The family left the synagogue together and walked slowly home.
I'm starved, said Nathan.
So you'll eat, said Frieda.
I'm hungry, too, said Rachel.
Well, you'd better not eat too much, Nathan said. *You're getting too fat.*
I am not. Mother, am I getting too fat?
You're just right.
She is too getting fat.
Stop teasing her, Frieda said.
It's the truth.
That's enough, snapped Hymie.

The children were taken aback by their father's reprimand. Their mother did all the scolding...a burden Frieda bitterly resented.

They walked the rest of the way home in silence. The dinner was eaten in comparative silence.

Every time Hymie passed the radio on the sewing machine his eyes lingered on the unopened letter on top of it, and he sighed with impatience. If they could listen to the radio, why couldn't he open the letter? However, Frieda was the keeper of the flame and he wasn't about to argue with her.

The rest of the day went leisurely by. Some cousins and friends dropped in and Hymie and Frieda were busy entertaining them. In the evening Hymie and Nathan returned to the synagogue for the evening services.

Hymie hardly slept that night. Frieda tossed and turned as well.

The second day of Rosh Hashonah was overcast. It threatened to rain all day, but it never did. Hymie developed a violent headache.

In the early afternoon, after the services, Aunt Rose and Uncle Sam dropped in. They looked well and happy. Uncle Sam had found a customer for his place. The man had already given him a deposit and Uncle Sam was preparing to retire in November. They were planning a cruise to the Caribbean some time in November or December.

Jack paid the Benders a surprise visit. He came by himself and complained about everything. He was in fine vitriolic form. He insulted several of the cousins and made everyone uncomfortable. However, just before he left, he met his match. Tillie turned up with her younger son, Herbert (Morris was still recuperating from his operation.) and a battle royal took place. The insults flew back and forth. It was a technical decision, but Tillie did seem to come out on top. She was louder and earthier, which made up for lack of true wit. Under different circumstances Hymie might have enjoyed the encounter but, being as tense as he was, he had to retire to the porch to clear his head.

Frieda joined him to make sure he was all right. Hymie shooed her back into the house and assured her that he was, then set off for a walk around the block.

He walked up Nye Avenue to Wolcott Terrace and then turned left. He walked slowly, his mind a blank. There were too many things to think about. He passed the apartment building that housed Aunt Rose and Uncle Sam. He came to Renner Avenue and turned left. He had intended to turn left when he got to Goodwin Avenue and return to the house but he wasn't up to facing a house full of visitors. Before he knew it he had reached Bergen Street and he kept on going. It was beginning to get dark. Was it evening or was the sky just overcast? He walked until he came to Weequahic Park. The sight of the trees and the grass stopped him. He realized now that he would never get back in time for the final holiday service. Nevertheless he turned back and walked quickly.

What a stupid thing to do! To walk out on one's guests. Most of the way back home was uphill and Hymie's legs were beginning to ache.

By the time he got home it was dark. He ran up the steps of the front porch and opened the door. He was surprised to find that Frieda wasn't there at the window. The light was on in the kitchen and he could hear the radio. He found Rachel and Nathan at the kitchen table. Nathan was buried in a school book and Rachel was reading a story book.

Where's your mother? asked Hymie.

She went to shul, said Nathan.

Hymie glanced at the radio. The letter was still there, unopened. What the hell! It was dark already. The holiday was over. He picked it up and went into his bedroom, closing the door behind him.

He sat on the bed, tore open the envelope, unfolded the letter and read the familiar Jewish script. It was a long letter, full of family news and gossip. Things were going reasonably well and his mother seemed to be in a cheerful frame of mind. He read on and on. Nothing. Hadn't she received Frieda's letter? Had Frieda neglected to make things clear? Finally, at the bottom of the page, he came across his answer.

"I am sorry to hear about your trouble, Hymie. How I wish I could help you. But all my children are dear to me and I feel that, as long as my strength holds out, I must try and be of use to you all. You are constantly in my prayers, my dear, dear son. Please give my love to the children."

That was it. That was his answer.

The bedroom door opened and Frieda stood before him. Her face was pale and her eyes were like black coals. Hymie looked up at her. She looked at the letter in his hand and then at his face, and she knew at once. She went up to him, put her arms about him and drew him to her. He pressed his head against her belly, his arms clasped about her waist.

They remained that way for what seemed an eternity. They had never been closer. They finally released one another.

Don't worry, said Frieda.

Hymie smiled and said nothing. He stood up and they held each other again.

I've got to go, he said finally.

Must you?

I've got to look in. I haven't been there for two days.

Frieda smiled ironically as her husband left the room. Just when she had found the lover she had always dreamed about, she was about to lose him.

CHAPTER THIRTEEN

A LAST HOPE

The days slipped by. Yom Kippur, the Day of Atonement, came and went. October was now part of the past. November was here, flying by, day by day, hour by hour.

Hymie, in a dreamlike state, made no further attempt to find a substitute. Tillie's suggestion that he put an ad in the paper was ludicrous. And, as far as the customers and friends at the bar were concerned, he decided it was pointless. Johnny Notte stopped by regularly, but made no mention of their conversation. He did return the money he'd borrowed, a good part of it, at any rate.

The business continued to prosper and, if not for the terrible doom that lay in wait for them, life was generally pleasant for the Benders...except for the fact that Hymie was beginning to be plagued by headaches and he lived on aspirin.

Molly's brother had opened a grocery store in Connecticut and was doing very well. Jack was seriously looking for a store of his own. He scanned the newspapers daily and got in touch with several real estate agents.

Uncle Sam and Aunt Rose had to postpone their trip to the Caribbean. The man who was buying the building had run into some difficulty and needed another month to raise the second payment.

Morris's leg had improved after the operation and he was getting about with less pain. Tillie had still not fully forgiven Hymie for turning to their mother, but she was cordial to Frieda, and she invited the family over for Thanksgiving.

On a gloomy Thursday, November twenty-fifth, the Bender family piled into the maroon Chevrolet and drove to East Orange. The day was chilly and damp. It was too cold for rain. It would probably snow.

The telephone poles, the trees, the houses flew by as they drove through the deserted streets. Before he knew it Hymie was driving along Main Street in East Orange. He turned up Hilton street and the family trooped up the stairs of Fifty Two Hilton Street, a two family house and the home of the Kaufmans.

There was the drink before dinner with Morris, and the noise of the children, and the turkey dinner, and they were driving home in the dark and it was snowing.

And suddenly it was December.

Hymie racked his brain. How was he to stop this inexorable march to his doom? Adam was of no help whatsoever. Hymie suspected that he wasn't even concerned.

Two heavy snowfalls.

Hymie tried to imagine the world without him. What was to happen with "the place"? And his little brood? Who would throw coal in the furnace at home? Or take out the ashes? And the Chevrolet? What was to become of that? Frieda couldn't drive. At first he hoped that Adam might be there to look after things. But no, Adam was unsure of his fate. At any moment he might be forgiven and whisked back to wherever he came from.

Two weeks before the official onset of winter the weather suddenly became very pleasant. The snow melted. The sun shone. The sky was a clear, cloudless blue.

It was a Friday night. Johnny Notte came in later than usual. He took Hymie aside.

Could you get away for a while? he asked.

Why? What's wrong?

You remember Loretta, don't you, my sister-in-law, Eddies wife?

What about her?

She's in the hospital again. She has a bad heart. I don't know how long she's got, and she's asked for you.

You told her?

A couple of weeks ago. And she's asked to see you.

Hymie hung up his apron, told Adam he was leaving and followed Johnny Notte out the door. They got into Johnny's car, which was parked outside, and drove a short distance to the City Hospital.

Hymie's heart was pounding, and he tried not to get too hopeful. But why else would Loretta want to see him? He'd met her several times at "the place". She'd been there for a few of the parties. She'd been friendly enough, but that was it. Eddie was a patron, and friendly enough, but he wasn't as close as Johnny.

It seemed to take Johnny forever to find a parking place. Finally they got out of the car and walked toward the hospital.

The waiting room was empty. They went past the deserted reception desk to the elevators. Johnny pushed the button and they waited and waited and waited. Finally one of the elevator doors opened and Hymie followed Johnny into the car.

What he saw as the door slowly closed (or what he thought he saw) almost crushed his hopes completely. It was the man in the black suit with the goatee. Why was he there? Was it for Loretta? Was it for himself? But, after all, this was a big hospital.

The elevator stopped on the third floor and Johnny led Hymie through endless corridors. Hymie caught glimpses of patients through open doors...old men, young children, women of all ages, people of all colors. Illness seemed to have no prejudice.

Johnny stopped suddenly. At the end of the corridor a group of people were gathered in front of a room. A woman was weeping.

That's Loretta's room, said Johnny. *Oh, God!* And tears rolled down Johnny's face. *Oh, God!*

They continued down the corridor. Eddie was there, weeping unashamedly, as were several members of the family. Hymie offered his condolences. Two nurses and an attendant entered Loretta's room to prepare her to be taken away. Hymie felt he was intruding and said his good-byes.

Thank you for coming, said Eddie.

Hymie shook hands with him.

I'll take you back, said Johnny.

No, no. Don't bother.

You sure?

That's all right. I'll get a cab

I'm sorry, Hymie.

Thank you, Johnny.

Hymie left the mourning family and headed for the elevators. He lost his way and found himself in what was obviously a wing reserved for young children. A young girl lay asleep under a plastic tent, an oxygen machine next to her bed. A little boy, no more than two or three, was sitting up in a crib, playing with his toes. He looked perfectly healthy. In another room an emaciated little boy sat in a chair, staring into the distance. It was all so quiet, so antiseptic. No weeping. No complaints. He thought of his own children, healthy and strong. Only the minor disturbances common to most...measles, a fractured limb which quickly healed, the ordinary cold. And then Hymie realized how lucky he'd been to have all those good, healthy years.

He finally came to an elevator. It was not the one he had come up on, but he pushed the button anyway. The door opened and he stepped in. It was obviously a small service elevator. He pushed the button for the first floor. The elevator descended and the door opened.

This did not look like the street floor, but Hymie got out anyway. He walked down a corridor and found himself in a large ward filled with old women, apparently senile. Skeletal faces lay against white pillows. Spindly legs propelled emaciated bodies an inch at a time from one spot to another. At least I'll be spared all that, Hymie thought. He was tempted to go up to one of the old women and present his case. What did life mean to these empty shells? But something stopped him? Was it shyness? Was it pride? A nurse came up to Hymie.

Can I help you? she asked.

I'm trying to find my way out, said Hymie.

The nurse gave him directions.

He walked down a flight of stairs. Now which way? He came to a section which contained curtained off booths. The air was strong with antiseptic, but the area didn't look that clean, and there seemed to be a great deal of activity.

A middle-aged nurse walked by and snapped, *What are you doing back here? Have you filled out a report?*

Hymie looked at her blankly.

The waiting room is that way. That way, mister. And she walked away.

Hymie headed in the direction of the waiting room. He heard moans of pain and sharp commands. Sounds of struggle and someone falling to the floor. An intern came dashing out of one of the curtained booths and ran down the corridor. The front of his white coat was smeared with blood.

Son of a bitch! the intern muttered as he disappeared. Hymie smelled the stale stink of vomit.

Another intern came up behind him. *Are you Mr. Brown?* the intern asked.

Hymie shook his head.

The young intern continued on his way, calling for Mr. Brown.

Mr. Brown suddenly appeared. He was a short, stocky black man in his fifties. He limped toward the young intern.

Yes sir? said Mr. Brown.

Come with me, said the intern and the two men disappeared behind the curtain.

At the end of the corridor was a waiting room, a large shabby room with worn chairs and benches. It was almost filled. Some people were seated. A few were standing around listlessly. The majority of the people were black.

There was a young mother, holding a child to her breast. Her left eye was badly bruised and she seemed to be in a daze, ignoring the baby's whimpers.

A fat old lady sat in another chair, flanked by two young girls. The woman was breathing hard and perspiring. One of the girls kept mopping the woman's brow with a handkerchief. The other girl was fanning the air in front of her with a newspaper.

A young man sat clutching his thigh. His leg was wrapped in a white, blood-soaked rag. The young man moaned softly under his breath.

The outside door of the waiting room was opened and a white-coated attendant entered supporting a man clutching his face. The man's head and hands were covered with blood. The attendant escorted the injured man through the waiting room and into the rear partitioned section.

Hymie sat down on an empty chair and looked about him. A well dressed young lady came up to him.

Have you filled out a form? she asked.

I'm not sick.

Are you here with someone?

I was visiting someone and I got lost, mumbled Hymie. He rose and started for the outside door.

Are you sure you're all right?

Yes, yes. I'm fine.

Hymie opened the door and found himself in a driveway. There was an ambulance parked nearby and a few feet away was an electric sign which read Emergency.

Hymie walked down the driveway, onto the sidewalk. He didn't know what street he was on. He was not familiar with this section of town.

He walked aimlessly, engrossed in his thoughts. He had resigned himself to accepting the inevitable, but Johnny Notte had revived his hopes. There might be someone who was actually willing to help him. All those people in the hospital. He should have approached one of them. Should he go back? Perhaps, if he explained to one of the nurses... It was madness. Why would anyone give up their life for a complete stranger? But mad or not he resolved to return to the hospital and present his dilemma to the first likely prospect.

He tried to retrace his steps but by now, he was lost. What a desolate part of town!

A woman was coming down the street in his direction. She wore high heels and carried a small sequined purse. It was a young, attractive colored woman, her face heavily painted.

Hello, Honey, she said. *You don't happen to have a match, do you?*

Hymie shook his head. He was hardly aware of what she was saying.

How'd you like to have a good time? I mean really nice.

Hymie shook his head and moved on.

Go fuck yourself, said the young woman and sashayed down the street.

Something in the tone of the voice made Hymie look back at the retreating figure. It was a man. He was sure of it.

The air grew chillier and a soft, fine rain began to fall. He passed a vacant lot. Toward the rear of the lot were some small shacks and a makeshift tent. There was a fire burning. He was tempted to approach the fire to warm himself.

Suddenly, from nowhere, two figures sprang forward, one behind him and one in front of him. He felt something in his back...a gun or a knife. A black man in his thirties stood in front of him, pointing a revolver at him.

Okay, Buddy. Let's have it. All your money. And don't try anything funny.

Hymie felt the pressure in his back. It was a knife.

Well? This time there was a note of uncertainty in the voice.

Hymie stood looking at the black man, growing angrier and angrier. This, indeed, was the last straw. Before he knew what he was doing Hymie kicked behind him with all his might. He heard a groan as he leapt forward. The gun went off in the air and he and the man in front of him, fell to the sidewalk in a life and death struggle. Hymie fought like a madman, pummeling the black man with his fists.

Okay, man. Okay, the black man whimpered and managed to pull away from Hymie and limp down the street. The second man was nowhere in sight.

Hymie picked up the revolver and fired it into the air several times until it clicked empty. He threw the gun away and staggered down the street, tears of anger and frustration streaming down his face as he ran.

He felt a sharp pain in his hand and saw that his left fist was all scraped and bleeding. There was a dull ache in his right thigh and in the small of his back. He leaned against a tree. Each breath he took was painful.

How long had he been running? Where was he? A dog passed by and snarled at him, baring his teeth. Hymie's hair stood on end. He snarled back at the dog and made a threatening gesture. The dog jumped back, snarled once more and continued down the street.

Hymie clung to the tree and fainted.

When he came to, he found himself lying in the mud at the foot of the tree. He was soaking wet. He rose painfully, clinging to the rough bark for support. The drizzle had stopped, but the air was chillier than ever.

He walked unsteadily down the dark streets. He'd lost all sense of direction. He walked for what seemed like hours. The houses about were shabby and dilapidated. Some of them were boarded up.

He finally came to a street that was well lighted and looked a little more prosperous. There were several stores on the block and some parked cars.

Hymie saw a cab coming slowly towards him. The off-duty sign was lit, but he waved at it anyway. The cab stopped. The driver was white, a tough looking middle-aged man. He looked Hymie up and down.

Where you going? he asked.

Nye Avenue.

Where's that/

It's in Newark. The Weequaic section.

Lemme see your money.

Hymie heaved a sigh, reached into his pocket and pulled out some bills.

Okay. Hop in.

Hymie climbed into the cab and it started off.

You'll have to give me directions when we get there.

I'll tell you, said Hymie and leaned back against the seat, shivering with the cold.

Where to now, Buddy?

Hymie woke with a start. He looked out the window. They were at Clinton Place and Clinton Avenue.

Turn left till you come to Nye Avenue, and then left again.

The driver followed Hymie's instructions and in a matter of minutes they were in front of the house. Hymie pulled out his money, gave the driver a healthy tip and climbed out of the cab. The driver thanked him and drove off.

He could see Frieda's figure at the darkened window. He walked
up the front stairs. Frieda was at the door to meet him.

What happened to you?

It's a long story.

You're soaking wet. Take off your clothes. You'll take a hot bath.

I'm all right now.

Take off your clothes.

Frieda went into the bathroom and ran hot water into the tub.
Hymie followed her and began to undress.

You're soaking wet. What happened to your hand?

I scraped it.

Hymie was down to his underwear. He hesitated. Frieda looked
at him.

If it's too hot, let some cold water run. And she left the
bathroom, closing the door behind her.

He removed his underwear, let some cold water run and stepped
into the tub. He soaked in the soothing water and luxuriated. Even the
burning hand didn't bother him.

There was a knock at the bathroom door. *Are you all right?*
Frieda asked through the half opened door.

I'm all right, said Hymie.

He made a half-hearted attempt at washing himself, then rose,
stepped out of the tub, reached for a towel and proceeded to dry himself,
then let the water out of the tub. The bathroom door opened slightly and
Frieda's hand came through, holding Hymie's pajamas.

Here's your pajamas, she said. She returned a moment later with
his slippers.

After he'd donned his pajamas and stepped into his slippers he
opened the door. Frieda came in, gathered up the clothes and threw the
washables into the hamper.

Hymie got into bed.

You want something to eat? asked Frieda.

Hymie shook his head.

Frieda turned off the light and got into bed. Hymie moved close
to her, sighed and rested his head on her breast. She placed her arm
around him and they spoke softly. Hymie told her what had happened
and Frieda listened attentively.

Take tomorrow off, she said. *At least the morning. It's
"Shabbas". You'll take it easy.*

All right, he murmured and he fell asleep, his head resting on his wife's breast.

Frieda sat quietly. She'd made up her mind. Actually the decision had been made some time ago.

CHAPTER FOURTEEN

FRIEDA

The following morning was Saturday. Frieda was up at the crack of dawn. Actually she'd been up for most of the night, planning. There was much to be done.

She closed her bedroom door very quietly, then checked the phone numbers in the pad next to the phone. It wasn't there. She got out the phone book. Kopanski, Kopanski. There it was. Frank Kopanski. 50 Hermon Street. It was almost seven o'clock.

It was Saturday and they might be sleeping late, she thought, but no matter. She picked up the phone and dialed. It rang three times. Four. Five. She was about to hang up when a sleepy voice came over the receiver.

Hello?

Frank? This is Frieda. Mrs. Bender. Hymie's wife.

Yes, Frieda? Is there anything wrong?

I'm sorry to wake you. But could I speak to Adam, please?

Just a minute.

A moment later Adam's voice was heard. *Hello?*

Adam, it's Frieda. Mrs. Bender. Hymie left the car at the store. Could you bring it up here before you open?

I'll bring it right over.

Thank you.

She hung up, her heart beating rapidly. She had taken the first step. Would she have the courage to follow through?

Forty five minutes later she was standing at the window when the maroon Chevrolet pulled up in front of the house. She ran quickly out of the house and down the stairs so that she could catch Adam before he got out of the car.

When the car came to a halt Frieda opened the front door and joined Adam on the front seat. She didn't want to risk talking in the house.

Is Hymie all right? asked Adam.

He's still asleep.

Would you like me to take you some place?

No.

Adam waited. Obviously the woman was excited, overwrought perhaps, and needed time to collect herself. When she finally did speak there was a quiet determination in her voice.

I'm going to take his place.

I beg your pardon? said Adam. Actually he'd heard her words loud and clear, but he wanted to make sure, because they were words he didn't want to hear.

I've thought a long time, Frieda continued. *But there's no other way. I want you to make the arrangements.*

There was a pause.

Can you make the arrangements?

Does Hymie know this?

I don't want him to know, until afterwards.

Do you think that's fair?

What do you mean?

I mean...it's his life.

Here was a situation Adam did not want to deal with. His job was to serve Hymie. But is this what Hymie would want? Probably not. Now what was she saying?

I don't understand, Frieda was saying.

I don't think this is what he'd want.

Is that important?

What is?

The children.

Don't you think they need their mother?

They need someone to provide for them even more, and I couldn't do that. Being a parent...

The words came pouring out. Where were they coming from? They felt so strange to her tongue and yet they were coming from her. She was saying them. And then she remembered. She remembered the Rabbi's sermon, a sermon she had heard many years ago.

BEING A PARENT IS THE MOST WONDER THING A PERSON CAN BE. IT'S A GIFT FROM GOD. IT'S A SACRED TRUST.

She was pregnant with Nathan at the time. She had stored those memorable thoughts in her mind, but it wasn't until she had held her baby in her arms, that beautiful, helpless miracle, that these words revealed their true meaning and became embedded in her heart. They were no longer words. They were a faith, a credo...a dedication that pervaded her whole being. No matter what she did from here on in, this infant, this enchanted bundle of life, was what she was put on earth for...this marvelous creation torn from inside her was her reason for living. Just as marriage had completed her as a woman, motherhood had completed her as a human being.

Adam sat studying this lovely creature, this Jewish madonna. She seemed to be surrounded by an unearthly glow. Was she a fellow cohort? He recalled all the great martyrs and heroines he had encountered down through the centuries. He knew how angry and how hurt Hymie would be and yet he couldn't see himself defying this force of nature.

Please! she was saying.

He'll be angry with me.

You mustn't tell him.

He'll know eventually.

Leave that to me.

Adam sighed.

You'll make the arrangements? Adam?

I'll make the arrangements.

When?

I'd better do it right away. I've been getting a lot of pressure.

Thank you. Hymie's going to take the day off, Frieda continued. *If that's all right. He needs the rest.*

Fine.

Do you know how to get back? You take the number 14 Bus...

Yes, I know.

Thank you, said Frieda. *You'll excuse me now. I have things to do.*

Yes, of course.

Frieda got out of the car and went back into the house.

Adam sat in the car. The more he thought about Frieda the more frightening she became. So fragile and yet so strong. He got out of the car and stood on the sidewalk trying to collect his thoughts, trying to organize his morning.

The sun was up but it did nothing to alleviate the greyness of the day. The street was quiet. Not a soul in sight. People were probably still asleep. This world was too much, too much, too much. How much longer, oh Lord? How much longer? He walked toward the bus, contemplating with great reluctance his dreary errand.

In the house Frieda made some phone calls then gave the children breakfast. She hustled Nathan off to the synagogue. He departed very reluctantly. At least he had the movies to look forward to in the afternoon, and his friend, Harold, would be joining him in shul, which made the ordeal easier to endure.

Rachel went into the front room and settled down with her doll and her picture book.

Frieda went into the bedroom. Hymie lay in bed fully awake.

How are you feeling? she asked.

So, so, Hymie answered.

Actually he was feeling quite well, considering what he had gone through the night before. His hand throbbed a little. He felt a slight ache in his thigh and some of his muscles were a little sore, but other than that, he felt fine. Not even a sniffle after all that exposure to the wet and the cold.

There's still time, if you wanna go to shul, said Frieda.

Thank you, no. thought Hymie.

Adam was here. He brought the car. I told him you wouldn't be in this morning.

Hymie said nothing. He sighed and looked about dreamily. Frieda pulled up the window shade. The sky was overcast. It looked like it might snow. Frieda stood at the window, looking out into the backyard.

Fanny's coming over this morning, she said.

Who?

Fanny. Fanny Friedman. She called a little while ago.

How is she doing?

Wonderful. I admire her.

When did Joe die?

It's almost a year now. And she looks marvelous. Of course, they didn't have any children. But even so, she's a strong woman. A very fine woman.

She talks a little too much.

So she likes to talk. But she has a heart of gold. Are you gonna stay in bed all day?

I wouldn't mind.

So sleep. It's quiet.

Where are the children?

Nathan went to shul. Rachel's in front.

I might as well get up, said Hymie and he started to get out of bed.

I'll warm some coffee, said Frieda and she went into the kitchen. (It was yesterday's coffee heated in a pan placed on a burner that was kept lit all through the Sabbath. You couldn't turn on the gas on the Sabbath.)

Hymie washed, dressed and had his breakfast. It seemed strange to be home on a Saturday morning. Pleasantly so. After breakfast he walked into the front room where he found Rachel playing with her doll.

What are you doing? he asked.

I'm taking my doll to the hospital.

What's the matter with her?

She has no appetite. I think she needs an operation.

Would you like to go for a walk?

All right.

Get your coat.

Rachel got up and ran into the kitchen. *Mommy, Mommy, I'm going for a walk with Daddy. Where's my coat?*

A few moments later the child returned with her coat and hat. Hymie helped her dress then went into the bedroom to get his coat.

Where are you going? asked Frieda.

I'll get a paper. You need anything? Hymie asked.

No, she replied. *Bundle up good. It's cold out.*

It was cold out, and a light snow had begun to fall.

Where are your gloves? Hymie asked his daughter as they walked up Nye Avenue toward Clinton Place.

In my pocket, answered the child.

You better put them on.

Rachel put on her gloves.

They turned right on Clinton Place. The lights were on in the synagogue. The Sabbath service was still in progress. They continued on towards Hawthorne Avenue till they came to the candy store where the Jewish Forward was available. Hymie bought a copy of the Forward and the New York Daily Mirror, which he read regularly. "More Fighting In Abyssinia" Always a war. He looked down at the child.

Would you like some candy? he asked.

Could I have some bubble gum?

Hymie bought the child some bubble gum and they started back home. He looked across the street at the Hawthorne Avenue Grammar School, the school his children attended. On the windows were pasted colored figures made by the students. Most of the art work were Christmas decorations. Christmas already.

An acquaintance passed by and Hymie nodded to him. It was getting cold. He began to walk faster, but Rachel couldn't keep up so he had to slow down, and he took her hand. He'd never get used to it, being a father. When they got back home he found Frieda in the bedroom, lying down, fully dressed.

What's the matter? he asked.

I'm not feeling well.

What's the matter with you?

I've had a cold all week. I think I have a fever.

He felt her forehead. It was burning hot. *Maybe I better call the doctor,* he said.

It's Shabbas. Let's wait till tomorrow.

Tomorrow is Sunday.

If it's an emergency, he'll come.

You want something?

I'll be all right.

If you want something, call me, said Hymie and he left the bedroom, leaving the door slightly ajar.

He sat in the kitchen, reading his papers then went into the bedroom to check on his wife. She seemed to be asleep. At least her eyes were closed. When Nathan came home from shul Hymie went into the bedroom again. Frieda was awake.

So how are you feeling? he asked.

What time is it?

It's half past twelve.

Is Nathan back from shul?

He just got back.

You must be hungry.

I can wait.

The children must be hungry.

You want me to give them eat?

No, no. I'll get up. She sat up with some difficulty. *You wanna get me my sweater? I feel chilly.* She coughed slightly.

Hymie handed her the sweater and she put it on rather shakily. Hymie followed his wife into the kitchen where Nathan was sitting at the table reading the Daily Mirror. The boy looked up.

You look terrible, he said. *What's the matter with you?*

I don't feel well.

That's obvious. What's the matter with you?

I've had a cold all week.

I think we ought to call the doctor, Nathan said.

Eat first and then I'll see how I feel.

Frieda managed to serve the meal. She stopped several times and held onto the stove or a chair. She ate nothing herself.

Maybe you should eat a little soup, said Hymie.

Frieda sighed, poured herself some soup and sat down at the table in front of the plate. She took a couple of spoons of soup and then stopped.

I can't eat, she said.

I think we ought to call the doctor, said Nathan.

I'll lie down for a while and maybe I'll feel better. She rose from the table and walked slowly back to her bedroom.

Hymie and Nathan, with Rachel's help, cleared the table and did the dishes. When Hymie went into the bedroom to check on his wife her eyes were closed, but apparently she was not asleep.

Leave the dishes on the table, she said. *I'll put them away. You'll mix them up.*

You want me to call the doctor?

I feel a little better. Let's wait.

Hymie went back into the kitchen.

I was gonna go to the movies with Irving, said Nathan.

So go.

Are you gonna be home?

I'm gonna be home. You have any money?

No.

Hymie handed the boy some money, more than enough for the movies.

Thank you. You think she'll be all right?

She feels a little better. Go ahead.

Nathan got his coat and started out the door. *I'll come right home afterwards*, he said and walked out the back door.

Hymie returned to his paper and then walked restlessly about the house. It was still snowing. He went down to the cellar and put some coal into the furnace. After he washed his hands he went into the bedroom. Frieda opened her eyes as he entered.

So how are you feeling? he asked.

So, so. Did Nathan go to the movies?

Hymie nodded.

Did you give him money?

I gave him money.

He studied her flushed face. *You should eat something,* he said.

Maybe a little later. What's Rachel doing?

She's playing in the front.

Don't come too near me. I don't want you to catch it. She began to cough violently, a deep rasping cough. It took her a while to recover.

I think I should call the doctor.

All right.

Hymie looked up the doctor's number and got the nurse on the phone. The doctor wasn't in at the moment but she expected to hear from him shortly and he'd call Hymie back.

The doorbell rang as Hymie hung up the phone and he went to the front door. It was Fanny Friedman, a small, dark cheerful woman in her mid thirties.

Hello, Hymie, she said. *What are you doing home?*

I took off. How are you?

Gott sei danke. Where's Frieda?

She's in bed. She isn't feeling so good. I called the doctor.

What's the matter?

It's a bad cold.

Rachel came into the dining room where the two of them were standing.

Hello, darling, said Fanny and she kissed the child. *Such a beautiful child. Where's your brother?*

He went to the movies.

Ah leben au deine koppele. Fanny turned to Hymie. *How long has she been sick? I talked to her this morning and she sounded fine.*

She got worse a little while ago.

I won't stay too long. Fanny took off her coat. *Maybe I can do something. Did you have your lunch?*

We ate already.

Did Frieda eat something?

She tried to eat some soup, but she couldn't finish it. I'll take your coat.

Hymie took Fanny's coat and hung it in the dining room closet.

Maybe I can make her something, said Fanny and she went into the bedroom. She came out shortly. *I'll make a little tea for her. That's all right. I'll find it.* Fanny went into the pantry and came out with the tea. She heated some water, produced a cup and sugar and lemon and moved about the kitchen as if it were her own. She took the tea into Frieda and after a while she returned with the empty cup. *She wants to talk to you.*

Hymie went into the bedroom.

It's so dark in here, he said.

Don't put on the light, said Frieda. *Pull up the shade a little.*

Hymie pulled up the shade furthest from the bed, overlooking the backyard. The room was still dark, but, at least, he could make out Frieda's form on the bed. Her face looked flushed. Hymie pulled up a chair and sat beside her.

How are you feeling? he asked.

So,so, she said and there was a pause. *Hymie, I wanna talk to you.*

Something in the tone of her voice made him apprehensive.

I talked to Adam this morning, she continued. *He said he'd make the arrangements.*

Arrangements? What arrangements? What are you talking about?

Don't get excited. Let me finish,, please. We've got to think of the children. I could never raise them by myself. How would we live? What would I do?

Frieda seemed to be shivering from the cold and Hymie felt a chill pass through his own body.

Are you listening to me?

I'm listening.

Mrs. Newman can look in on the children. And I'm sure Fanny would be glad to help out. Maybe she could even stay here for a while. It doesn't have to be Fanny, but she's a very nice woman, and since she lost Joe she's all alone.

And me? What about me?

You'll find someone, Hymie. It doesn't have to be Fanny.

Hymie's eyes filled with tears. His mind whirled about. He didn't know what to say. He didn't know what to do. He wouldn't allow it. He couldn't allow it!! But did he have the power to stop it? And did he have the right? The children, the children! Everything for the children. That's all she thought about. That's all she lived for.

What are you thinking? she asked.

Why does it have to be you?

Is there anyone else?

We've still got time.

Hymie...?

Yes? What is it?

When you find someone... I beg of you, let it be someone who'll be a good mother. It doesn't have to be Fanny, but she's a very nice woman and she deserves a good life, and a good husband.

A compliment? On her deathbed, a compliment.

The phone rang. He was about to answer it when he heard Fanny's voice. She came into the bedroom a moment later.

It's the doctor, she said.

Hymie answered the phone. *My wife is very sick, doctor.*

What's the matter with her? The doctor sounded tired and irritated.

She's got a fever and she's shivering.

Is she coughing?

Very badly. It sounds terrible.

I'll be over in half an hour, said the doctor and hung up.

What did he say? asked Fanny.

He's coming over.

Good. I've got to go. I'm expecting someone. But if you need me, call me. Anytime. You hear? Anytime.

Thank you. I'll get your coat. And he helped Fanny into her coat.

I'll take a look at Frieda before I go. And Fanny went back into the bedroom. When she came out she said, *There's plenty of food in the ice box. You'll stay home? I mean you won't go into the store?*

I'll be here.

Can you give the children supper?

I'll manage.

She'll be fine. The doctor'll give her something and she'll be up in no time. I'll call you later.

Thank you, Fanny.

Fanny went into the front room to say good-bye to Rachel and Hymie saw her out the door. After Fanny left he went into the front room.

Are you hungry? he asked his daughter.

We just ate. Is Mommy still sick?

The doctor's coming.

Do you think she'll need an operation?

I don't know.

Should I make her some soup?

She just had some tea?

But soup is better.

Maybe later. It's dark in here, he said and turned on the floor lamp.

It's Shabbas. You turned the light on on Shabbas.

So God'll punish me, Hymie muttered and walked into the kitchen. He looked around, trying to remember. What was he gonna do? It came back to him. He picked up the phone and dialed "the place". Adam's voice came over the phone.

Why didn't you tell me? Hymie asked.

Hymie?

Why didn't you tell me?

She asked me not to.

I won't have it. Did you hear what I said?

I heard you. Hymie, I've done everything I can for you.

But...

What's done is done. Hymie, listen to me. We can't always have what we want. You should know that by now.

But...

I've got to go. And Adam hung up.

He stood next to the phone, angry and confused. He heard Frieda's voice, calling him. It seemed to come from far off. When he went into the bedroom Frieda said, softly, *Hymie, please. It's the only way. For the sake of the children.*

The children, the children! and he wept bitterly. Always the children. How could he go on without her? She was half of him. He was half of her. What identity did he have without her? She was the foundation of his life...his mind, his heart. In some ways she was weak, it's true. But it was her very weakness that made him strong. And, perhaps, in the long run she was really the stronger of the two.

We've had our chance, said Frieda.

The doorbell was ringing and Hymie went to answer the front door. It was the doctor, black satchel in hand.

Well, at least the snow's stopped. But it's cold as hell out there.

Let me take your coat, said Hymie, following the doctor into the dining room. Rachel stood watching the two men, her doll in her hand.

Hello, little girl. What's your name?

Rachel.

Would you like a lollypop, Rachel?

Rachel nodded shyly.

Say please and it's yours.

Please.

Do you like lemon? he asked, and she nodded. The doctor took a lemon lollypop from inside his jacket pocket and handed it to the little girl.

What do you say? Hymie heard himself say. Was he becoming the mother and the father already?

You're welcome, said the doctor. He patted Rachel's head and started toward the rear of the house. *Wait here,* he said to Hymie and disappeared into the bedroom, closing the door behind him.

Hymie sat down at the kitchen table and waited. Rachel came into the kitchen, doll in one hand, the lollypop, still wrapped, in the other.

Is the doctor going to operate? she asked.

No.

Then why did he bring his satchel?

He's going to examine her.

Then is he going to operate?

He's not going to operate!

Hymie's tone silenced the child. After what seemed like hours, the doctor finally emerged from the bedroom.

Your wife is a very sick woman, he said. *She should be in a hospital. Only the hospital I'm connected with has no beds right now. I'm going to order an oxygen tank. She's got to have one.*

Anything.

And she should have a nurse. I know someone I can call.

Call her, please.

Where's your phone?

Hymie showed the doctor the phone and the doctor made two calls. The oxygen tank would arrive the following morning. The nurse would come at ten that night and would stay until eight in the morning. The doctor gave Hymie a prescription for some medicine that Frieda should start at once. Two tablespoons every three hours.

How long has she been this sick?

Since this morning/

Hmm. It usually takes days. Keep her well covered, and if there's any change, let me know. I'll drop by in the morning.

What is it, Doctor?

Pneumonia. We'll keep on top of it, but it's serious.

Thank you, Doctor, said Hymie and he followed the doctor into the dining room, got the doctor's coat out of the closet and helped him into it.

Get that prescription filled right away. And she should have some nourishment. Soup, hot cereal. Cream of wheat, preferably. Anything

that's easy to digest. I'll see you tomorrow. And the doctor walked out
the front door.

Hymie went back into the bedroom. It was so dark he could
hardly see his wife, so he turned on the overhead light. It was a very
dim one, but he could see Frieda clearly and what he saw frightened
him. Her face was even more flushed than before. Her eyes glistened
strangely, and she was breathing with great difficulty.

I'm going to get the medicine, he said. *Will you be all right?*

Frieda nodded and Hymie took his coat out of the bedroom
closet.

Hymie...? Frieda whispered.

He turned to her and she beckoned him towards her. He
approached the bed and leaned over.

Not too close, she cautioned, and he backed away. She was dying
and she was still giving orders. *Call Jack. I want to see him.*

I'll call him when I get back.

Shut the light.

Hymie turned off the bedroom light and left the room. As he
entered the kitchen the back door opened and Nathan bounded in, his
cheeks red with cold.

How is she?

Take this prescription to the drugstore.

Shall I wait for it?

Tell them we need it right away.

Shall I wait for it?

Yes, yes.

Nathan ran out the door, prescription in hand.

Hymie sighed and went back into the bedroom to return his coat
to the closet. *I sent Nathan to the drugstore with the prescription. I'll
call Jack now,* he said. Frieda said nothing. There was just the labored
breathing.

He pulled the chain in the foyer and turned on the overhead
light. Way was it so dark? It's so early in the day. He looked up Jack's
number and dialed. Molly answered. She was surprised to hear Hymie's
voice. Jack wasn't home. He told her about Frieda's illness and she said
she would have Jack call as soon as he got in. After he finished talking
to Molly, Hymie went back into the bedroom. *You want something to
eat? What did you say?* (He could hardly hear her.)

No.

The doctor said you should eat something.

Later.

The phone rang and Hymie answered it. It was Tillie.

Oh, it's you, she said. *Where's Frija?*

She's in bed. She's sick.

What's the matter with her?

She's got pneumonia.

Pneumonia?!

That's what the doctor said.

You had the doctor?

He ordered an oxygen tank and there's a nurse coming tonight.

I'll be over in the morning. Call me if you need me. You hear?

Yes, I hear.

He hung up and went into the kitchen and sat at the kitchen table. So helpless! What is there to do? This couldn't be happening. This was the one alternative he'd never dreamed of. She had defied her stepfather to marry him, but had she ever really loved him? The phone rang and Hymie answered it. It was Jack.

What's the matter? he snapped.

Frija's sick. She's got pneumonia.

How sick is she?

I said, she's got pneumonia.

All...right, all right.

She asked me to call you.

I just...got in.

You don't have to come now.

I-I've been...working all day. There were...some back orders to...fill.

I said you don't have to come now.

So...why did you call me? I won't...sleep all night.

Hymie slammed down the phone and started for the kitchen when the phone rang again, and it was Jack. *I'll...come tomorrow. First thing.*

All right. So you'll come tomorrow.

And Hymie hung up. He heard Frieda's voice calling him and went into the bedroom.

Who was that? she asked.

It was Jack. He's coming tomorrow morning.

Frieda sighed and turned away.

Hymie heard the kitchen door opening and went to meet Nathan, who had a small bag in his hand.

You forgot to give me money, the boy said.

Did he give you the medicine?

Here it is. I said I'd be right back with the money.
How much is it?
A dollar ninety eight.

Hymie handed Nathan the money and the boy dashed off. Hymie read the directions on the bottle, then got a teaspoon and went into the bedroom. Frieda swallowed the red liquid and then lay back and closed her eyes.

Did you give the children eat?
Not yet.
Can you manage?
I'll manage. Don't worry.

Hymie went into the kitchen, put the cap back on the medicine and placed it on the sink. He proceeded to serve the evening meal. He thought he knew where all the dairy utensils were kept, but at this point, what did it matter? The food and the dishes were on the table when Nathan returned from the drugstore, and the three of them sat down to eat. It felt strange eating at the kitchen table without Frieda moving about.

Hymie helped with the dishes. Nathan washed and he and Rachel dried. They heard a shuffling noise in the bedroom and Hymie went to investigate.

Frieda was walking slowly across the room.

Where are you going? Hymie asked.

The bathroom, she replied.

Hymie supported her and Frieda shuffled into the bathroom.

I'll be all right, she said and closed the bathroom door behind her. She opened it a few minutes later and Hymie helped her back into the bedroom and into the bed. She lay exhausted on the pillow and Hymie pulled the covers over her. *I'll be all right.* She seemed delirious.

When would that nurse get here? Maybe he should call the doctor.

She doesn't look too good, said Nathan. *What did the doctor say?*

He ordered an oxygen tent, and a nurse.

She must be very sick.

She's very sick.

Rachel began to cry.

Stop crying, snapped Nathan. *That's not going to make her any better.*

All right, all right, said Hymie.

Rachel stifled her sobs and sat forlornly on a chair.

What is it? Did the doctor say? asked Nathan.

Pneumonia.

Pneumonia?! That's serious.

Is Mommy gonna die?

No, she's not gonna die! Not yet, at any rate, said Nathan.

Later on the children turned the radio on softly, huddled around it and listened to their favorite programs.

Frieda tried to eat some toast and tea that Hymie had prepared for her. She managed a few bites of the toast and a few sips of tea, then sank back exhausted.

Fanny Friedman called at nine o'clock to see how Frieda was doing, and said she'd come by in the morning.

At nine thirty Hymie sent the children to bed. He sat in the kitchen, at the table doing absolutely nothing. He didn't want to listen to the radio. He'd read the paper, not that he could really concentrate on what he was reading. The minutes ticked by.

At ten to ten the front doorbell rang and Hymie admitted the nurse. She was an efficient, motherly looking woman with a slight Viennese accent. She made Frieda comfortable, bathed her face, arranged her pillow and fussed over her. She persuaded Hymie to go to bed.

He took off his shoes and his shirt, and lay down on the daybed in the dining room. The nurse said she'd wake him about an hour before she was ready to leave. He lay on the day bed wide awake. He started to get up to tend to the furnace, but then remembered that Nathan had taken care of it. He thought about calling Adam, but he realized it would be pointless. What's done was done. Besides, that's what she wanted. And maybe she was right. Maybe the burden would have been too much for her. He fell into a state of semi-sleep and started to dream. Strangely enough it was his own funeral that he dreamed about. He walked beside his own casket and saw himself lowered into his grave. He got up, what he thought was a few hours later, to go to the bathroom. The nurse was sitting in the kitchen, knitting.

She's asleep, she said.

Is she any better/

About the same. The fever has got to break sometime soon.

Then you think she'll get better?

Let's hope so, said the nurse and returned to her knitting.

Hymie went to the bathroom, returned to the daybed and finally, in the early hours of the morning, he fell into a deep sleep. It was daylight when the nurse woke him. She was kind enough to get his breakfast for him while he shaved. She used the wrong silverware, but Hymie said nothing. As she was getting ready to leave she asked him if he'd be wanting her that night. He said he would speak to the doctor and let her know and that seemed to satisfy her.

She should be getting some oxygen, said the nurse.

The doctor ordered it, said Hymie.

After the nurse left he looked in on Frieda. Her breath was coming in hoarse gasps. Was she reaching the end? Should he call the doctor? But the doctor said he'd be coming by in the morning. Hymie looked in on the children. They were fast asleep.

The oxygen tank arrived a little after nine. The young man who brought it showed Hymie how to place the nozzle to Frieda's mouth and nose. It did seem to help her breathing. Hymie signed the slip for the tank and the young man left.

Nathan came out of his bedroom sleepily and asked how his mother was doing. Hymie lied and said she was feeling a little better. The boy went to the bathroom and then back to bed. An hour later the children got up and Hymie gave them their breakfast.

Tillie called and said she'd be there around noon. Jack arrived a little after eleven. Hymie took his coat and Jack went directly into the bedroom. When he came out his face looked ashen.

She's...dying, said Jack.

The children looked at him wide-eyed.

Shhh, said Hymie. What a stupid thing to do, in front of the kids!

Where's...the doctor?

He'll be here soon. You want some coffee?

I need...a drink.

At this hour?

S-s-since when...are you so particular. Give me a drink.

Hymie poured Jack a drink and then put the bottle away

M-molly sent her regards. Nathan...has a stomach ache, so... she couldn't come. 'Oy, Gottenyu!' sighed Jack and his eyes filled with tears. *She's so young.*

Is Mommy gonna die? asked Rachel.

No, no, no. She's gonna be all right, said Hymie and he gave Jack a murderous look.

The doctor arrived a little before noon, looked Frieda over and took Hymie aside. *There's nothing more to be done,* he said. *We'll know by tonight.*

Is she in a coma? asked Hymie.

No, said the doctor. *But she's very weak.*

There's...nothing you can do? asked Jack as he joined them.

I'm afraid not, the doctor answered.

This is my brother-in-law, said Hymie.

She's my sister.

I'm sorry.

Th-that and a token...

I've got to be going. Call me if there's any change.

Sh-sh-shouldn't she be in a hospital?

Even if I could find her a bed, at this point it would be too dangerous to move her. The doctor put on his coat and left.

S-s-some doctor!

He's a good doctor.

And...he's just...gonna let her die? This is nineteen...thirty three. P-people don't die from pneumonia.

Jack, shut up, please.

All right, all right. I won't...say another word. I'll just...sit here and watch...my sister die.

Hymie clenched his fist and said nothing.

An hour later Tillie and Morris arrived. Tillie took off her coat and handed it to Hymie and went into the bedroom. Morris shook hands with Hymie and Jack.

I'm sorry, said Morris.

Sh-she's not...dead yet, snapped Jack.

Morris limped over to the dining room table and sat down. Hymie left the two men and went into the bedroom. Tillie was bathing Frieda's face with a damp cloth. Frieda seemed to be unaware of what was going on.

You want something to eat? Tillie asked Hymie.

No.

Have the children had their lunch?

Not yet.

You sure you don't want anything?

I'm not hungry.

Tillie left the bedroom and Hymie sat down next to the bed. Frieda's eyes were closed and she looked lifeless. He heard her call his name. Her lips were moving but he couldn't hear what she was saying. He leaned over.

The children, she whispered. *Bring...the children.*

He rose and went into the kitchen. Tillie was preparing the lunch and Nathan and Rachel were sitting at the kitchen table.

Your mother wants to see you, he said.

The children looked at him wide-eyed and followed him into the bedroom. They stood silently at the side of the large double bed. Rachel started to lean over to kiss her mother, but Frieda held up her hand to prevent it. She held the little girl's hand and patted it. Nathan reached out and his mother held his hand for a moment then, squeezed it gently. Rachel began to cry softly. Frieda withdrew her hand and lay quietly. Hymie led the children back into the kitchen where he found Jack and Morris in whispered conversation with Tillie.

Shall we go in? asked Tillie.

Hymie nodded and the three adults followed the grieving husband into the dying woman's room. They all stood at the bedside looking down at Frieda, who seemed to be unaware of their presence. Jack tried unsuccessfully to stifle his sobs. Hymie knelt beside his wife and took hold of her hand. *Frija,* he pleaded. *Don't leave me.* He buried his head in the covers and wept. The room was silent except for Hymie's helpless sobs. After a few moments Hymie pulled himself together and looked up.

Frieda's eyes were wide open. Was she dead or alive? She blinked.

Frija? Hymie whispered.

She smiled weakly at him. *I had a terrible dream*, she said softly.

How do you feel? he asked.

Hungry.

I'll get you some soup, said Tillie and she left the room.

It was a miracle.

Jack, what are you doing here? asked Frieda.

I...came to...pay you a visit. Wh-wh-what are you doing in bed?

I'm tired. I need a rest. She noticed Morris standing nearby and tried to say something but the effort was too much for her.

You shouldn't talk too much, said Hymie.

We'd better let her rest, said Morris and he limped out of the room, followed by Jack. Hymie sat beside the bed and held his wife's hand. Tillie entered with a bowl of soup.

Go in the other room. Let me feed her.

Hymie leaned over and kissed Frieda's hand. She smiled weakly at him and he left the room. As he entered the kitchen the children came over to him.

Is Mommy gonna be all right? asked Rachel.

She's gonna be fine, he said. He leaned over and kissed the little girl, then he kissed the boy. He placed his arms about them both and pulled them towards him in an emotional embrace. As he held his children it crossed his mind, for the first time, that if his wife had died he would have been left alone with them. How would he have coped? How would they have behaved towards him?

He released the children and started for the front room where he could hear Jack and Morris conversing, but he changed his mind. He wanted to be alone for a moment.

He turned around and went into the children's bedroom, closing the door behind him. He sat on Rachel's bed and looked out the window, over the radiator into the yard across the way. It was snowing lightly and the sky was gray. The radiator hissed as the steam escaped. The room was warm, yet Hymie felt a chill. What was going to happen now? Winter was just a few days away. Had Adam intervened again? Was he still doomed?

He heard the phone ringing. It startled him but he resisted getting up to answer it. Somehow he knew that the answer to all the questions whirling about in his mind would be answered by that phone call. The bedroom door opened.

It's Aunt Rose, said Nathan. She wants to speak to you.

Hymie rose slowly from the bed, walked to the phone and picked it up apprehensively.

Hymie, said Aunt Rose. Her voice was trembling. *Sam is dead.*

I'll be right over, said Hymie, and he hung up. Uncle Sam was dead. How? Why?

What's wrong? asked Nathan.

Uncle Sam isn't feeling well.

Must be an epidemic.

Yes, said Hymie, and he smiled ironically. He went to get his coat out of the bedroom closet. Frieda was finishing the bowl of soup. *Where are you going?* she asked.

It's Uncle Sam. He's not feeling well. He avoided Frieda's eyes. She looked at him questioningly. *Is he...?*

Hymie nodded.

When?

I don't know. Aunt Rose just called.

Tell her I'll be over a little later, said Tillie.

Hymie nodded and put on his coat as he walked into the front room where Morris and Jack were sitting.

Wh-where are you...going?

Uncle Sam just died.

He was sick for a long time, said Morris.

Hymie walked out the front door, down the steps and onto the street. It was snowing lightly. He walked slowly around the corner onto Wolcott Terrace, breathing in the cold air, the soft flakes brushing against his face. Uncle Sam was dead. He'd taught him how to tend bar, how to mix drinks, how to shmooze with the customers. He'd helped him with his English. Actually he was the first real friend he had here in America.

Hymie entered the lobby of the apartment building and pressed the button marked "Bender". The door buzzer rang. Hymie entered the hallway, took the elevator, which was there waiting for him and rode to the fifth floor.

The door to the apartment was ajar and, as he entered, Aunt Rose came to meet him. Her pretty face was puffy with weeping. He put his arms about her. She clung to him and started to cry, then pulled herself together and heaved a sigh. *Do you want to see him?* she asked. He nodded.

Aunt Rose led him into the bedroom, looked at her husband for a moment then walked out of the room. Uncle Sam lay on his bed in his blue silk pajamas. His eyes were closed and his skin looked slightly yellow, but the expression on his face was that of peace.

Hymie studied the still figure on the bed with mixed emotions. He had had his differences with his uncle. The man had been both kind and stubborn, whimsical and sober...but never cruel, and never deliberately thoughtless. He had been a good man and a good husband, and now he would never have the children that he and Aunt Rose had wanted so badly. I was the only son he ever had, thought Hymie. Had he sacrificed himself for me?

Aunt Rose appeared in the doorway and Hymie joined her in the living room. They sat on the elegant sofa in the lamplight. Hymie looked about the room. Uncle Sam would never enjoy this beautifully furnished apartment again.

The doctor sent for the ambulance, said Aunt Rose. *They should be here any minute. I would like you to do me a favor, Hymie. I don't have anyone. Would you take care of the arrangements for me?*

Of course.

We have a plot. If you call Mr. Goldfarb, or maybe the funeral director. I guess the nearest funeral parlor would be Richters. They're on Clinton Avenue.

Do you want me to call them?

In a minute. She produced a note. *He left me this note. It's personal, but I think you ought to know. He had an operation once for cancer, a long time ago. For a while he was doing all right and then it came back again. Recently he seemed to be doing fine but then last week... This afternoon he called Adam. Sam was never a very demonstrative person but I want you to know that he loved you very much.* She began to weep and Hymie put his arm around her and they sat on the sofa for several minutes.

The buzzer rang and Aunt Rose got up. *That must be the ambulance*, she said and went into the foyer to push the button. Two attendants came in with a stretcher and Aunt Rose ushered them into the bedroom. While they were preparing to take Uncle Sam away Hymie got on the phone and arranged for Richters to handle the funeral.

After the body had been removed Aunt Rose sat on a chair looking lost and very small.

I wanna go over to Richters now and make the arrangements, said Hymie. *Do you have anyone to stay with you?*

I'll be all right, said Aunt Rose.

I hate to leave you alone.

That's all right. I can go next door to my neighbors.

Hymie bent over, kissed Aunt Rose on the cheek and left the apartment. He walked back to his house. Morris and Jack were still in the front room. Tillie was in the kitchen, watching the children eat their dinner.

I have to go to the funeral parlor, said Hymie. *I left Aunt Rose all alone.*

We'll go over right now, said Tillie. *Will Jack be here till you get back?*

I'm sure he'll stay, said Hymie and he started toward his bedroom.

She's asleep, said Tillie.

Hymie went into the front room. Jack readily agreed to stay until he returned and Hymie left for the funeral parlor.

Richters was an attractive stone building, beautifully landscaped. Hymie pushed the doorbell and was ushered across the plushly carpeted lobby to Martin Richter's private office where arrangements were made to bury Uncle Sam the following day at one o'clock. He called Aunt Rose from Richter's office. Tillie and Morris were there. He arranged to pick up Aunt Rose the following day at noon.

When he got back home he found Fanny Friedman getting ready to leave. Jack left soon afterwards. Frieda was still asleep. At six o'clock Mrs. Newman came downstairs to help with the evening meal. Frieda woke up, ate some soup and a roll, went to the bathroom and promptly fell asleep again.

The children listened to the radio and were sent to bed. After Hymie called Adam to tell him he would not be in the following day he got into his pajamas, prepared the day bed in the dining room, lay down there and fell into a deep, dreamless sleep.

CHAPTER FIFTEEN

THE FUNERAL

The following morning was bright, cold and clear. Hymie woke up in time to help the children with their breakfast and see them off to school. He put some coal in the furnace, noticed that there was very little coal left in the bin and made a mental note to remind Frieda to order some coal.

Frieda woke around nine o'clock. He prepared breakfast for her and served it to her in bed, much against her will. He drove to Hawthorne Avenue and did some light shopping...bread, butter, milk, eggs and a few cans of vegetables.

The doctor arrived a short time later, pronounced Frieda well on the way to recovery but cautioned her to take it easy for a few days. Hymie arranged for Mrs. Newman to give the children their lunch and left to pick up Aunt Rose.

Aunt Rose greeted him at the door of her apartment. She wore a dark dress, a shawl over her head and no make-up. She looked like a little old lady. Hymie helped her on with her coat and they left for the funeral parlor.

A handful of people appeared to pay their last respects. Tillie and Morris were there; Uncle Sam's sister, Aunt Esther, and her husband, Uncle Izzy, some cousins, Uncle Sam's bartender and a couple of close friends. The service was held in the small chapel. The rabbi's remarks were brief...almost abrupt, Hymie felt. He could have said a little more than that. But then maybe that's the way his uncle would have wanted it.

The ride to the cemetery was a long one. It was on the outskirts of town, the cemetery that belonged to the Congregation Agudath Israel, Hymie's congregation. Hymie was given the honor of throwing the first shovelful of dirt onto the coffin. Then all the men pitched in. Even Morris limped forward to contribute his bit. The rabbi said a few, final words and the funeral was over. That was it.

Tillie and Morris had to get back to the store. The others rode back to the apartment where Aunt Rose provided some refreshments.

Hymie was reluctant to leave Aunt Rose but her sister, who'd flown in from Rochester, would be spending the night with her. Aunt Rose's future plans were up in the air. She'd probably stay with her sister for a while. She seemed to be holding up remarkably well.

It was late afternoon when Hymie got back home. Frieda was up and about in the kitchen, preparing the evening meal. She was in her bathrobe and Rachel was helping her. When Nathan got back from Hebrew school they all sat down at the kitchen table. Frieda was pale, but she did seem to be gaining strength rapidly. After supper Nathan and Hymie shooed her back to bed and, with Rachel's help, they did the dishes.

Later in the evening Hymie drove down to "the place". He was greeted by the customers like a long lost friend. Adam and Phil were behind the bar. Adam grinned broadly at him when he came in. Even Phil gave him a smile and a handshake. Hymie stayed for a couple of hours and was greeted warmly by Johnny Notte when he came in. Johnny offered his condolences for the loss of his uncle, but was happy that Hymie had survived the ordeal. He ordered a round of drinks for the house. Hymie got home much later than he'd planned, and in rather a wobbly condition.

By the first day of Chanukah, which fell on the day before Christmas, Frieda was just about fully recovered and Hymie took her down to Bergen Street to look for a dress. She had to have something decent to wear to May Bender's wedding. It took several trips...to Springfield Avenue, to Bergen street again...and finally Frieda found something she liked. She had lost quite a bit of weight and looked very slim and elegant in her new dress. Even Hymie, who never commented on her clothes, thought it was a very nice dress.

Hymie agreed, after seeing Frieda in her new dress, that he did, indeed, need a new suit. He protested, rather feebly, about going to Tillie's but he ended up getting a suit there and it was a nice one.

Now you look like a "mensch", said Tillie.

The wedding was quite a fancy one, at the Clinton Manor, an elegant pink stucco building surrounded by a large, well-kept lawn. It looked like a wealthy private home from the outside, which it had probably been originally. Hymie and Frieda had a minor tiff about the size of the check they should give as a gift. After all, said Frieda, they were just second cousins. But Hymie insisted on giving a sizable amount. He was not going to look cheap. The affair left a deep impression on Hymie and he thought it would be nice to have Nathan's Bar-Mitzvah party at the Clinton Manor.

You crazy? said Frieda. *You know how much this place costs? And besides, they're all booked up a year in advance.*

It wouldn't hurt to look into it.

Do as you please.

Which meant forget it. He saw that Frieda was getting edgier and edgier as the day of Nathan's Bar-Mitzvah approached. Frieda was about to lose her little baby, her first born, and he was sure she would take to her bed with her nerves. And sure enough as spring rolled by and summer came to an end Frieda was silent and morose. A very bad sign. Any sort of a celebration was out of the question. Even a small gathering at the shul on a Saturday.

So on a Thursday morning early in October Nathan took off from school and he and his father headed...rather surreptitiously, Nathan thought...down Nye Avenue to the Osborne Terrace shul. That was where Nathan went to Hebrew school.

It was a beautiful fall morning. The leaves had just begun to turn. Nathan read his portion of the Torah and made his little speech, first in Yiddish and then in English. There was liquor and honey cake and father and son left the shul with a rare feeling of comradeship. Hymie was proud of the boy, but chagrined at the modesty of the affair.

The following morning Hymie and Adam were alone in the place. Hymie was taking stock and Adam was rinsing out some glasses.

If you'd like to go on a vacation, said Adam, *This might be a good time. I don't know how much longer I'll be here.*

A vacation had never occurred to Hymie. However he mentioned it to his wife and Frieda seemed delighted by the idea. There was a long holiday week-end coming up and it was decided to take the children out of school for three days. Nathan wasn't too happy about that, but what the hell.

The summer season was over, but it was still warm and they made arrangements to stay at the Hotel Lorraine in Bradley Beach. Actually it was the first formal vacation Hymie had since coming to America, and the first vacation the entire family spent together. Hymie was lost and restless for the first couple of days, but he enjoyed the sea air. Frieda was as happy as a young girl. She loved the seashore, strangely enough since she had this phobia about traveling. And the children, of course, had a great time on the beach, playing with friends. Some families from their neighborhood were enjoying the final summer days.

Hymie returned to Fifty Bar and Grill tanned and healthy looking. That was on a Tuesday. Phil was off that night. The place was empty and Hymie told Adam that he could leave.

I'll close up, said Hymie.

The angel looked tired and rather worn. He took off his apron and hung it up. He looked about the room, sighed and turned to Hymie with a faraway look in his eye.

You're a good man, Hymie, he said. He kissed Hymie gently on both cheeks, turned and walked out through the swinging doors.

Adam was due to start work the following day at noon, but he never showed up. Hymie sent Phil upstairs to the Kopanski apartment. Maybe Adam had overslept. But Hymie knew what the report would be as soon as the bartender re-entered the saloon. Adam's room was empty except for his new suit, which was hanging in the closet.

NORMAN BEIM

PHOTO BY MARTY BEIM

About the Author

As an actor Norman Beim has appeared on Broadway in "Inherit The Wind" with the legendary Paul Muni, Off Broadway at Joe Papp's Public Theatre and he stood by for Van Johnson in the National tour of "Tribute". He continues to make occasional television appearances on "Saturday Night Live" and several "soap operas". Among his directing credits is a production of "Harvey" with Joe E. Brown. His plays have been produced in Holland, Belgium and at various theatres across the country and have won a number of awards. Mr. Beim is a member of the Dramatists Guild, Actors Equity, the Screen Actors Guild and AFTRA. "Hymie And The Angel" is his first novel.